GARFIELD & Co

BASED ON THE ORIGINAL CHARACTERS CREATED BY

JIM DAVIS

PAPERCUT Z ™

NEW YORK

GRAPHIC NOVELS AVAILABLE FROM PAPERCUTZ ™

GRAPHIC NOVEL #1
"FISH TO FRY"

GRAPHIC NOVEL #2
"THE CURSE OF
THE CAT PEOPLE"

GRAPHIC NOVEL #3
"CATZILLA"

COMING SOON:

GRAPHIC NOVEL #4
"CAROLING CAPERS"

GARFIELD & Co GRAPHIC NOVELS ARE AVAILABLE IN HARD-COVER ONLY FOR $7.99 EACH. AVAILABLE AT BOOKSELLERS EVERYWHERE.

OR ORDER FROM US: PLEASE ADD $4.00 FOR POSTAGE AND HANDLING FOR THE FIRST BOOK, ADD $1.00 FOR EACH ADDITIONAL BOOK. PLEASE MAKE CHECK PAYABLE TO NBM PUBLISHING. SEND TO: PAPERCUTZ, 40 EXCHANGE PL., STE. 1308, NY, NY 10005 (1-800-886-1223)

WWW.PAPERCUTZ.COM

GARFIELD & CO #3 "CATZILLA"
© 2011 PAWS INCORPORATED. ALL RIGHTS RESERVED. GAR-FIELD™ AND THE GARFIELD CHARACTERS ARE TRADEMARKS OF PAWS INCORPORATED.

BASED UPON "THE GARFIELD SHOW" ANIMATED TV SERIES, DEVELOPED FOR TELEVISION BY PHILIPPE VIDAL, ROBERT REA AND STEVE BALISSAT, ADAPTED FROM THE COMIC STRIP BY JIM DAVIS. A DARGAUD-MEDIA AND FRANCE 3 COPRODUC-TION. WITH THE PARTICIPATION OF CENTRE NATIONAL DE LA CINÉMATOGRAPHIE AND THE SUPPORT OF RÉGION ILE-DE-FRANCE. ORIGINAL STORIES BY MIKE PULEY (ORANGE AND BLACK), JIM DAVIS (UNDERWATER WORLD), AND MARK EVA-NIER, (PERFECT PIZZA, UNDERWATERWORLD).
© DARGAUD 2011 WWW.DARGAUD.COM
WWW.THEGARFIELDSHOW.COM

ORTHO - LETTERING AND PRODUCTION
MICHAEL PETRANEK - ASSOCIATE EDITOR
JIM SALICRUP
EDITOR-IN-CHIEF

ISBN: 978-1-59707-278-6

PRINTED IN CHINA
AUGUST 2011 BY O.G. PRINTING PRODUCTIONS, LTD.
UNITS 2 & 3, 5/F, LEMMI CENTRE
50 HOI YUEN ROAD
KWON TONG, KOWLOON

DISTRIBUTED BY MACMILLAN
FIRST PAPERCUTZ PRINTING

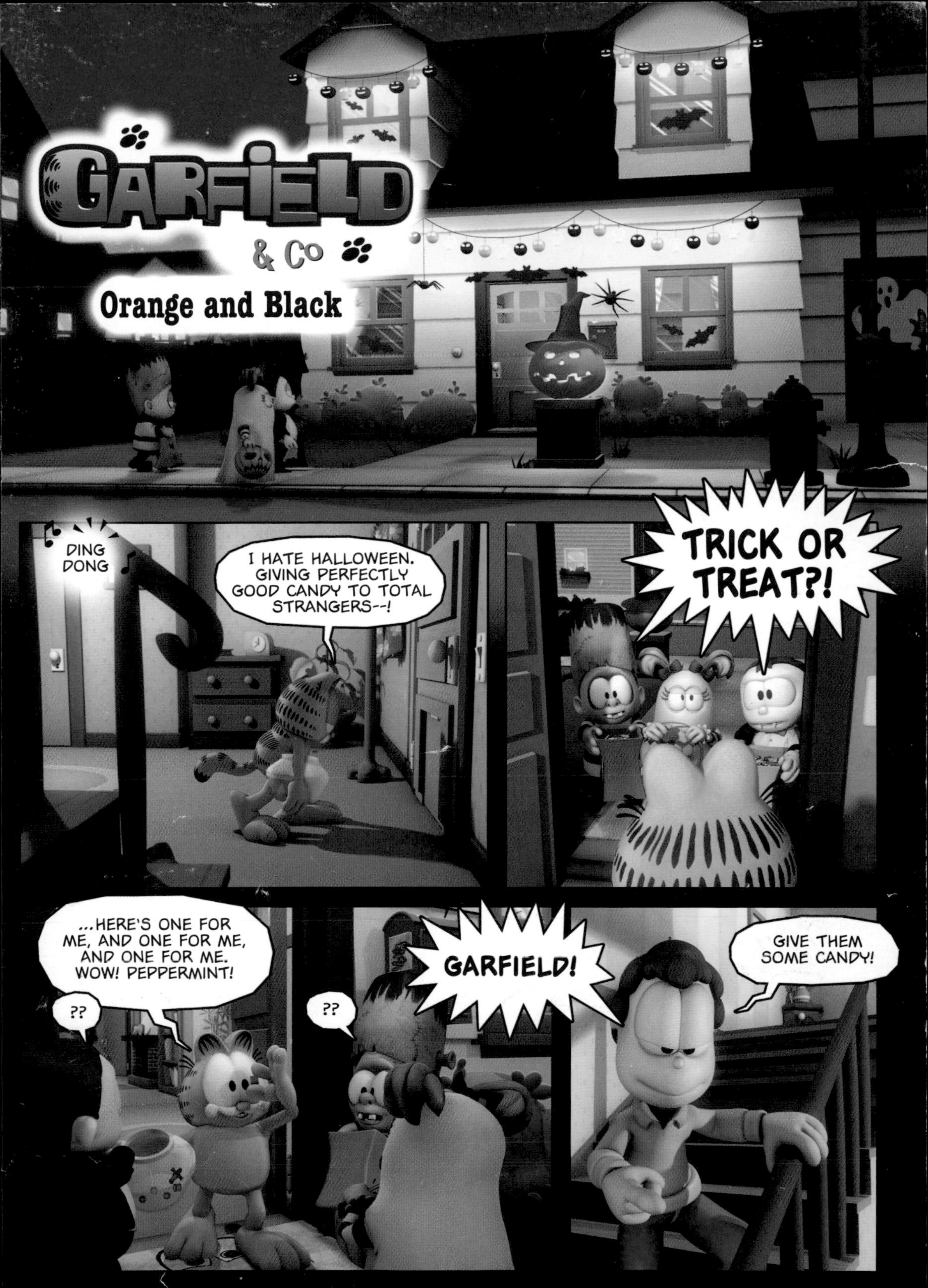
GARFIELD
& Co
Orange and Black
DING DONG
I HATE HALLOWEEN. GIVING PERFECTLY GOOD CANDY TO TOTAL STRANGERS--!
TRICK OR TREAT?!
...HERE'S ONE FOR ME, AND ONE FOR ME, AND ONE FOR ME. WOW! PEPPERMINT!
??
??
GARFIELD!
GIVE THEM SOME CANDY!

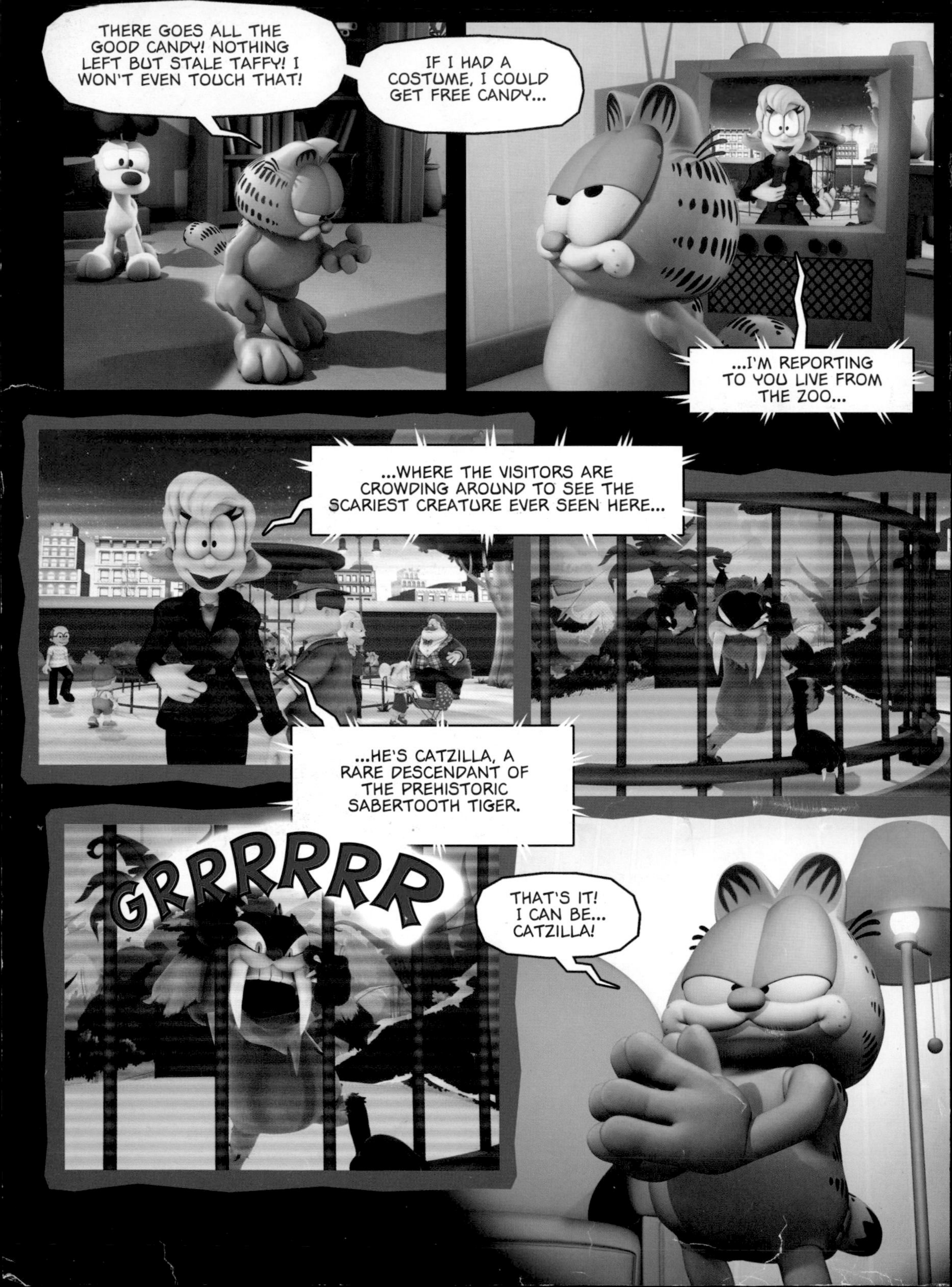
THERE GOES ALL THE GOOD CANDY! NOTHING LEFT BUT STALE TAFFY! I WON'T EVEN TOUCH THAT!
IF I HAD A COSTUME, I COULD GET FREE CANDY...
...I'M REPORTING TO YOU LIVE FROM THE ZOO...
...WHERE THE VISITORS ARE CROWDING AROUND TO SEE THE SCARIEST CREATURE EVER SEEN HERE...
...HE'S CATZILLA, A RARE DESCENDANT OF THE PREHISTORIC SABERTOOTH TIGER.
GRRRRRR
THAT'S IT! I CAN BE... CATZILLA!

THERE! A LITTLE PAINT.

I'LL BORROW THIS TOY'S TEETH.

PERFECT! I AM CATZILLA!

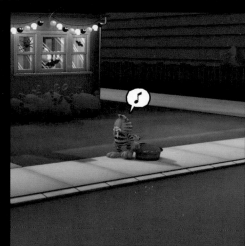

OH, MY GOSH! WHERE'S CATZILLA?

HE'S ESCAPED!!

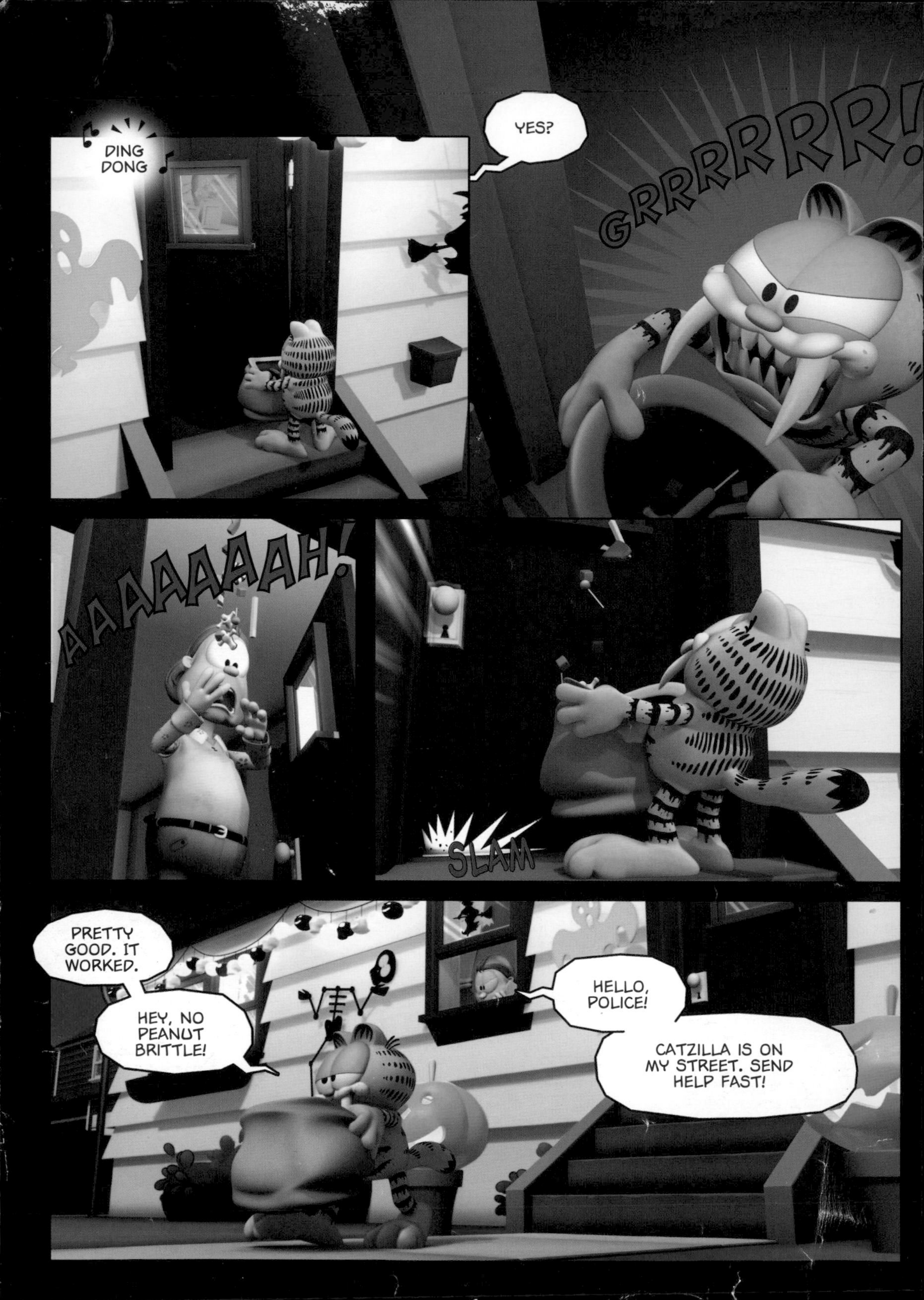
DING DONG
YES?
GRRRRRRR!
AAAAAAAH!
SLAM
PRETTY GOOD. IT WORKED.
HEY, NO PEANUT BRITTLE!
HELLO, POLICE!
CATZILLA IS ON MY STREET. SEND HELP FAST!

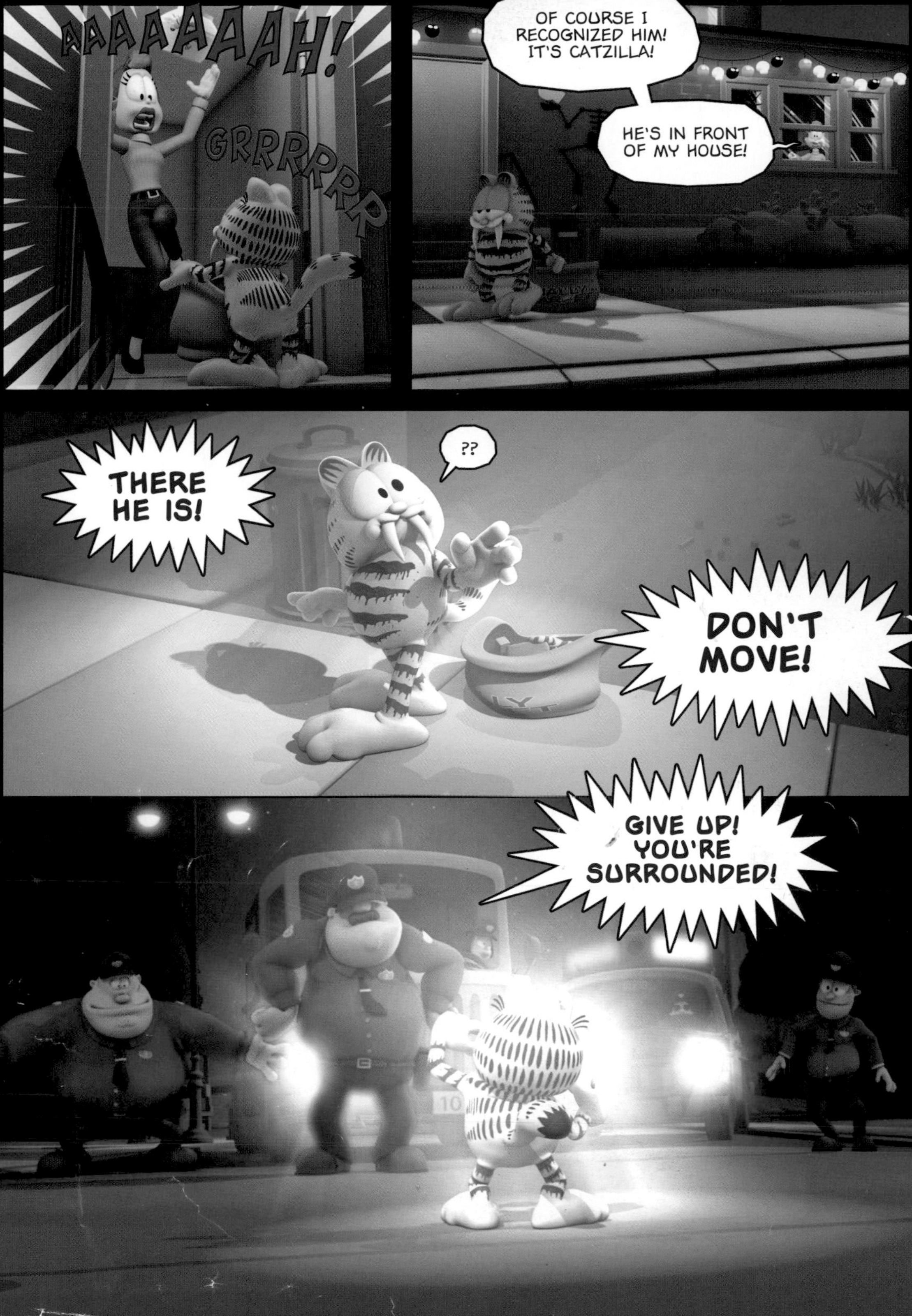
AAAAAAAAH!
GRRRRRRR
OF COURSE I RECOGNIZED HIM! IT'S CATZILLA!
HE'S IN FRONT OF MY HOUSE!
THERE HE IS!
??
DON'T MOVE!
GIVE UP! YOU'RE SURROUNDED!

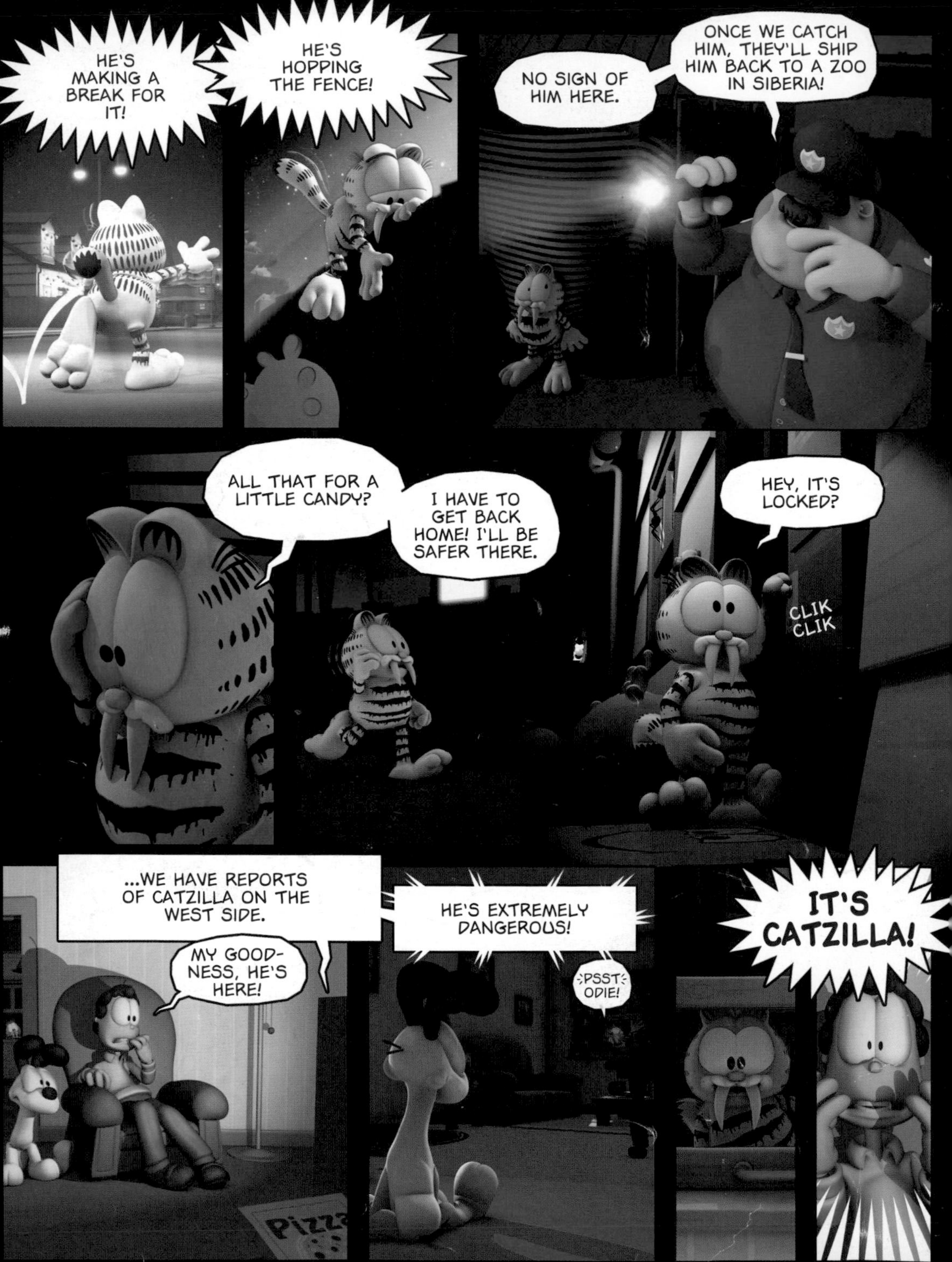

HE'S MAKING A BREAK FOR IT!
HE'S HOPPING THE FENCE!
NO SIGN OF HIM HERE.
ONCE WE CATCH HIM, THEY'LL SHIP HIM BACK TO A ZOO IN SIBERIA!
ALL THAT FOR A LITTLE CANDY?
I HAVE TO GET BACK HOME! I'LL BE SAFER THERE.
HEY, IT'S LOCKED?
CLIK CLIK
...WE HAVE REPORTS OF CATZILLA ON THE WEST SIDE.
MY GOOD-NESS, HE'S HERE!
HE'S EXTREMELY DANGEROUS!
PSST! ODIE!
IT'S CATZILLA!

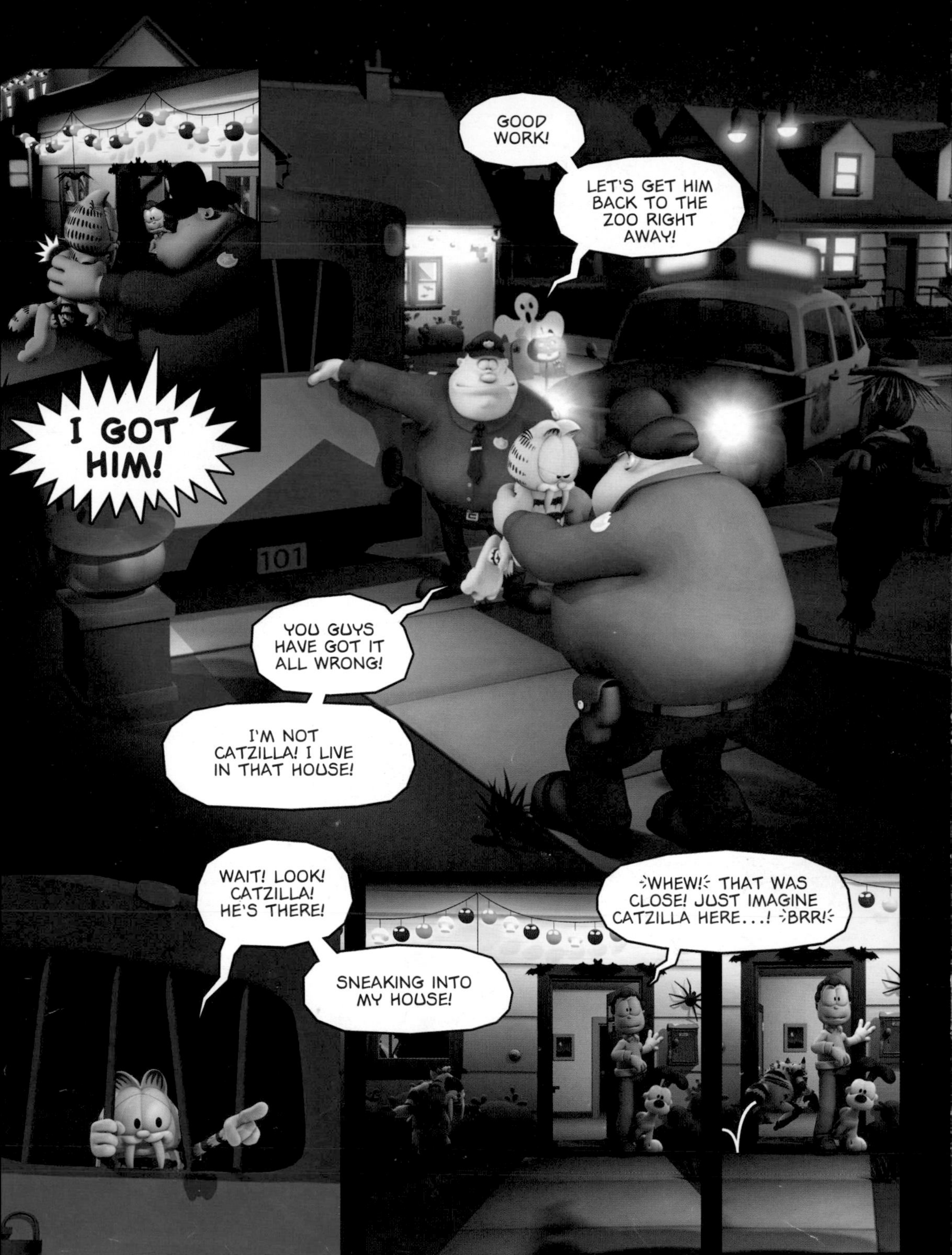
I GOT HIM!
GOOD WORK!
LET'S GET HIM BACK TO THE ZOO RIGHT AWAY!
101
YOU GUYS HAVE GOT IT ALL WRONG!
I'M NOT CATZILLA! I LIVE IN THAT HOUSE!
WAIT! LOOK! CATZILLA! HE'S THERE!
SNEAKING INTO MY HOUSE!
WHEW! THAT WAS CLOSE! JUST IMAGINE CATZILLA HERE...! BRR!

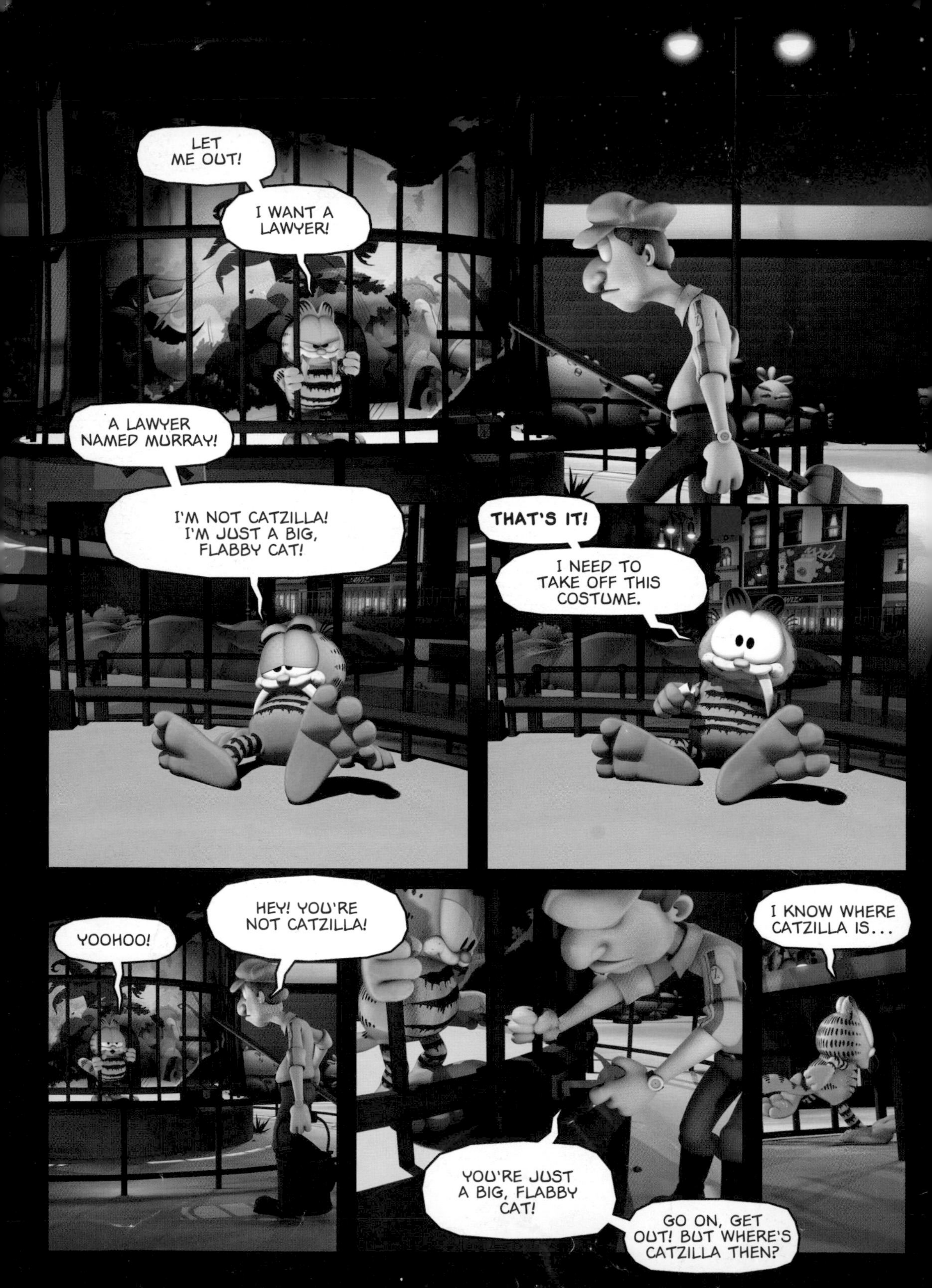
LET ME OUT!
I WANT A LAWYER!
A LAWYER NAMED MURRAY!
I'M NOT CATZILLA! I'M JUST A BIG, FLABBY CAT!
THAT'S IT!
I NEED TO TAKE OFF THIS COSTUME.
YOOHOO!
HEY! YOU'RE NOT CATZILLA!
YOU'RE JUST A BIG, FLABBY CAT!
GO ON, GET OUT! BUT WHERE'S CATZILLA THEN?
I KNOW WHERE CATZILLA IS...

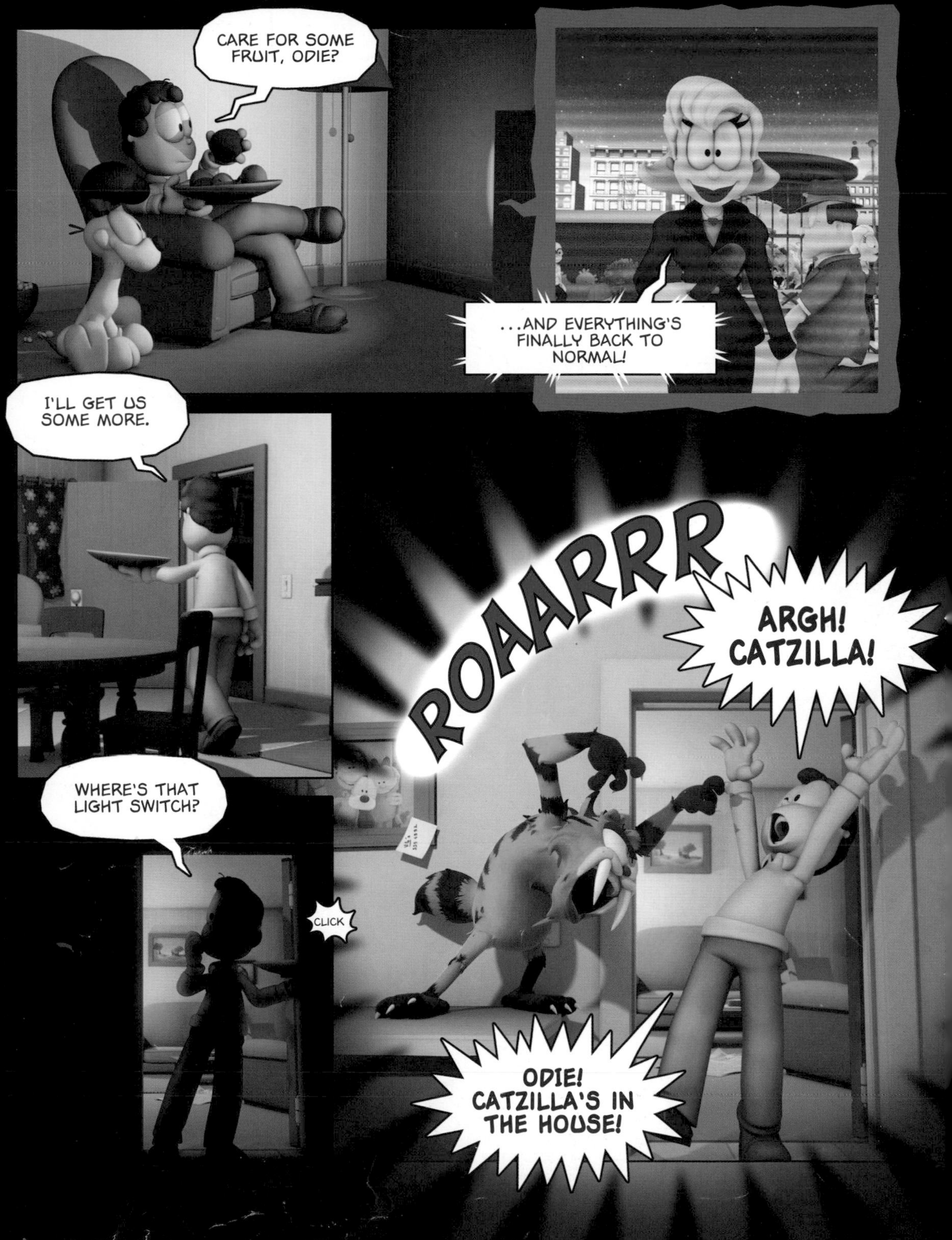
CARE FOR SOME FRUIT, ODIE?
...AND EVERYTHING'S FINALLY BACK TO NORMAL!
I'LL GET US SOME MORE.
WHERE'S THAT LIGHT SWITCH?
CLICK
ROAARRR
ARGH! CATZILLA!
ODIE! CATZILLA'S IN THE HOUSE!

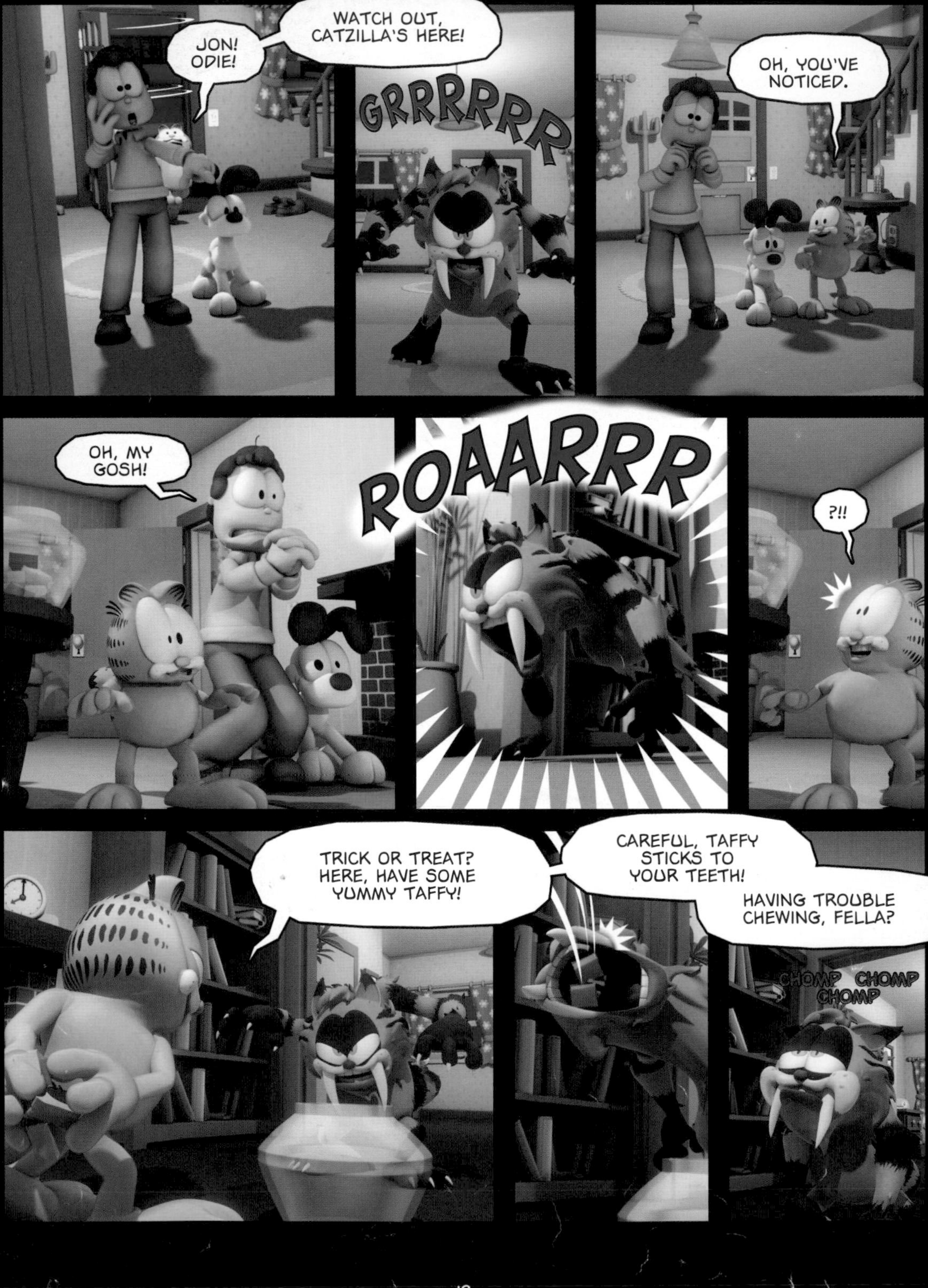
JON! ODIE!
WATCH OUT, CATZILLA'S HERE!
GRRRRRRR
OH, YOU'VE NOTICED.
OH, MY GOSH!
ROAARRR
?!!
TRICK OR TREAT? HERE, HAVE SOME YUMMY TAFFY!
CAREFUL, TAFFY STICKS TO YOUR TEETH!
HAVING TROUBLE CHEWING, FELLA?
CHOMP CHOMP CHOMP

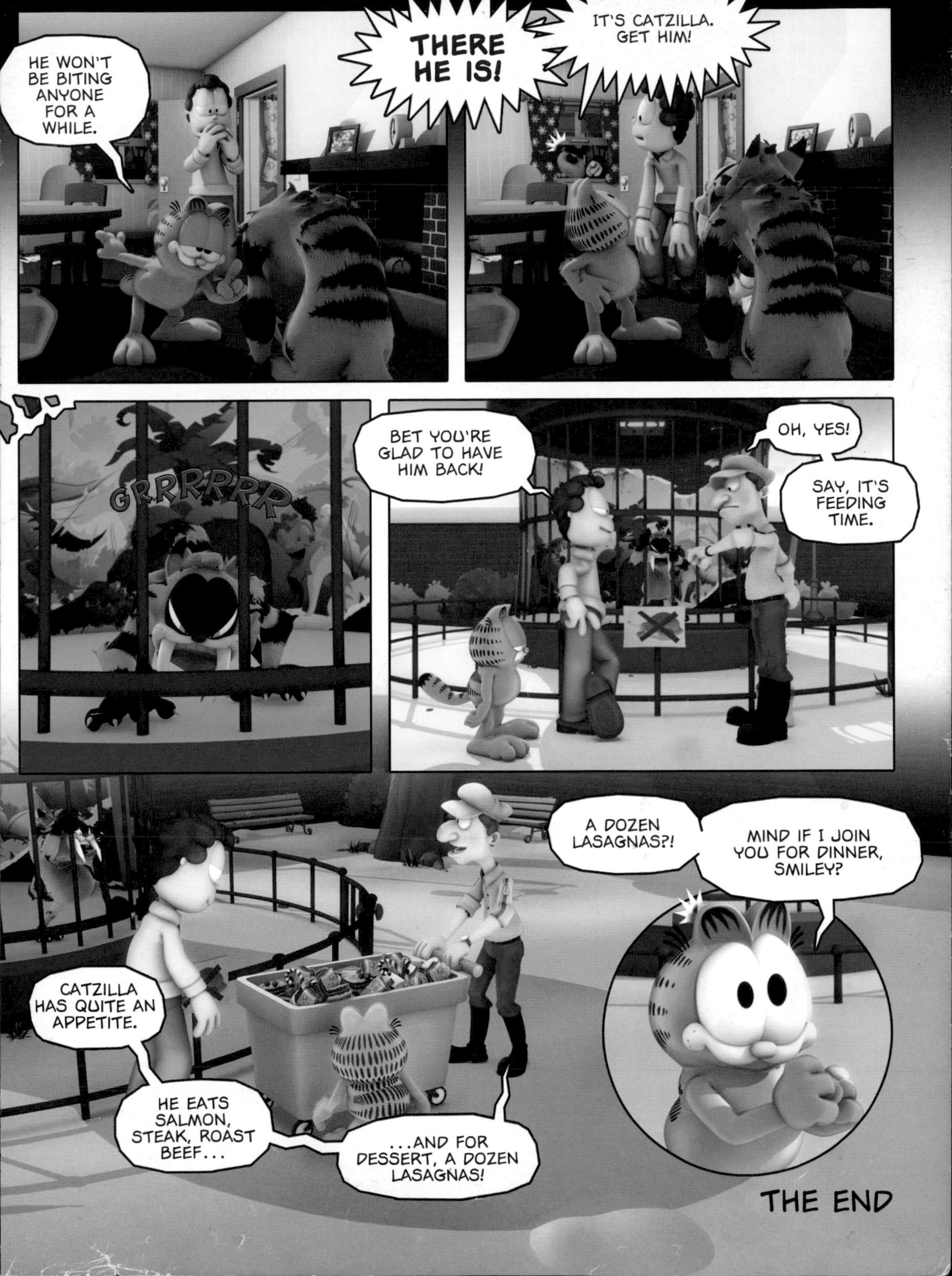
HE WON'T BE BITING ANYONE FOR A WHILE.
THERE HE IS!
IT'S CATZILLA. GET HIM!
GRRRRRR
BET YOU'RE GLAD TO HAVE HIM BACK!
OH, YES!
SAY, IT'S FEEDING TIME.
CATZILLA HAS QUITE AN APPETITE.
HE EATS SALMON, STEAK, ROAST BEEF...
...AND FOR DESSERT, A DOZEN LASAGNAS!
A DOZEN LASAGNAS?!
MIND IF I JOIN YOU FOR DINNER, SMILEY?
THE END

WATCH OUT FOR PAPERCUTZ

Welcome to the third GARFIELD & Co graphic novel from Papercutz. I'm you're lasagna-loving Editor-in-Chief, Jim Salicrup, with a special preview of an all-new Papercutz series coming your way in November! It's about a girl named Rebecca and her best friend, Ernest, who happens to be a germ…

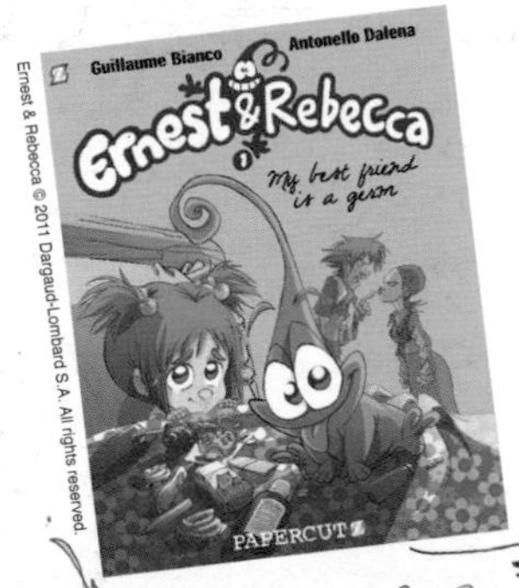
Guillaume Bianco
Antonello Dalena
Ernest & Rebecca
1
My best friend is a germ
PAPERCUTZ

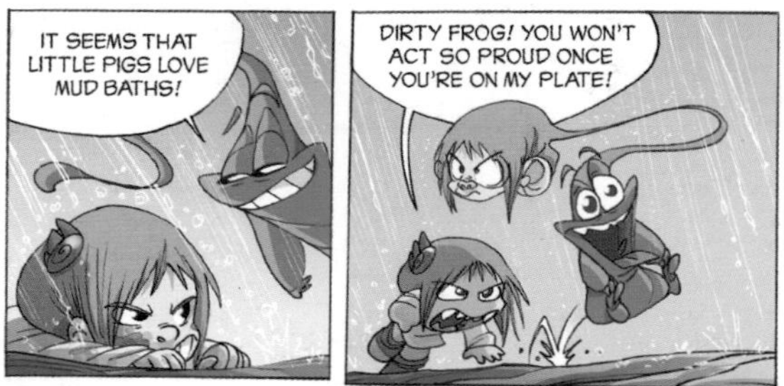
IT SEEMS THAT LITTLE PIGS LOVE MUD BATHS!
DIRTY FROG! YOU WON'T ACT SO PROUD ONCE YOU'RE ON MY PLATE!

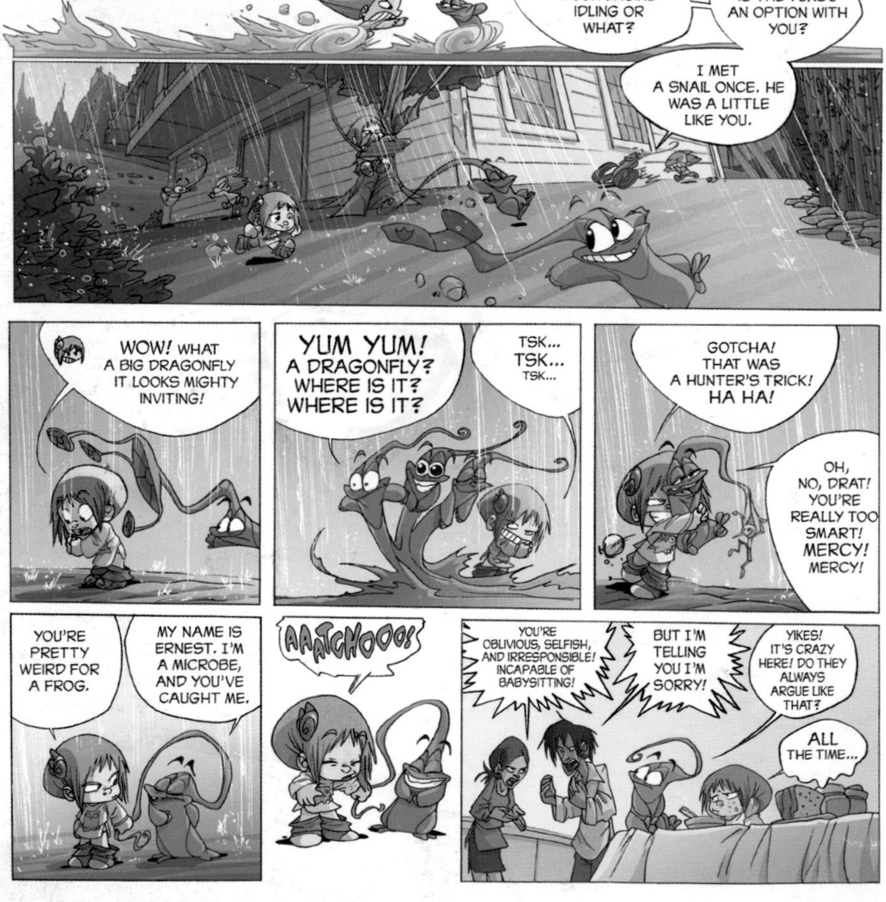
IS YOUR ENGINE IDLING OR WHAT?
IS THE TURBO AN OPTION WITH YOU?
I MET A SNAIL ONCE. HE WAS A LITTLE LIKE YOU.
WOW! WHAT A BIG DRAGONFLY IT LOOKS MIGHTY INVITING!
YUM YUM! A DRAGONFLY? WHERE IS IT? WHERE IS IT?
TSK... TSK... TSK...
GOTCHA! THAT WAS A HUNTER'S TRICK! HA HA!
OH, NO, DRAT! YOU'RE REALLY TOO SMART! MERCY! MERCY!
YOU'RE PRETTY WEIRD FOR A FROG.
MY NAME IS ERNEST. I'M A MICROBE, AND YOU'VE CAUGHT ME.
AAATCHOOO!
YOU'RE OBLIVIOUS, SELFISH, AND IRRESPONSIBLE! INCAPABLE OF BABYSITTING!
BUT I'M TELLING YOU I'M SORRY!
YIKES! IT'S CRAZY HERE! DO THEY ALWAYS ARGUE LIKE THAT?
ALL THE TIME...

Don't miss ERNEST & REBECCA #1 "My Best Friend is a Germ" on sale at booksellers everywhere November 2011! Uh-oh! I just barely have enough room to mention that coming even sooner to booksellers everywhere: GARFIELD & Co #4 "Caroling Capers" -- with three more festive episodes of our favorite fat feline. Don't miss it!

Till then, watch out for Papercutz! Jim

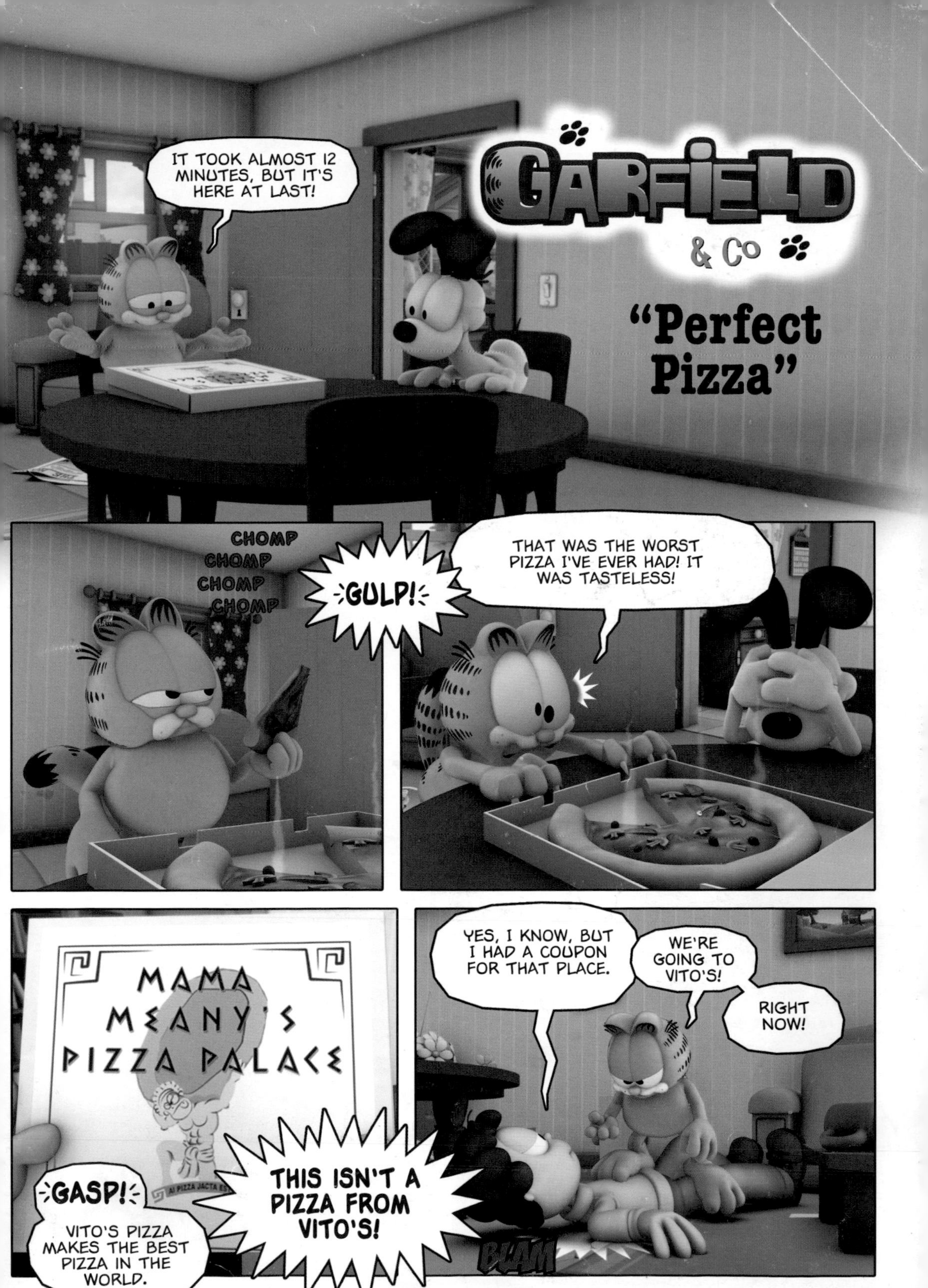
GARFIELD
& Co
"Perfect Pizza"
IT TOOK ALMOST 12 MINUTES, BUT IT'S HERE AT LAST!
CHOMP
CHOMP
CHOMP
CHOMP
GULP!
THAT WAS THE WORST PIZZA I'VE EVER HAD! IT WAS TASTELESS!
MAMA MEANY'S PIZZA PALACE
GASP!
VITO'S PIZZA MAKES THE BEST PIZZA IN THE WORLD.
THIS ISN'T A PIZZA FROM VITO'S!
YES, I KNOW, BUT I HAD A COUPON FOR THAT PLACE.
WE'RE GOING TO VITO'S!
RIGHT NOW!
BLAM

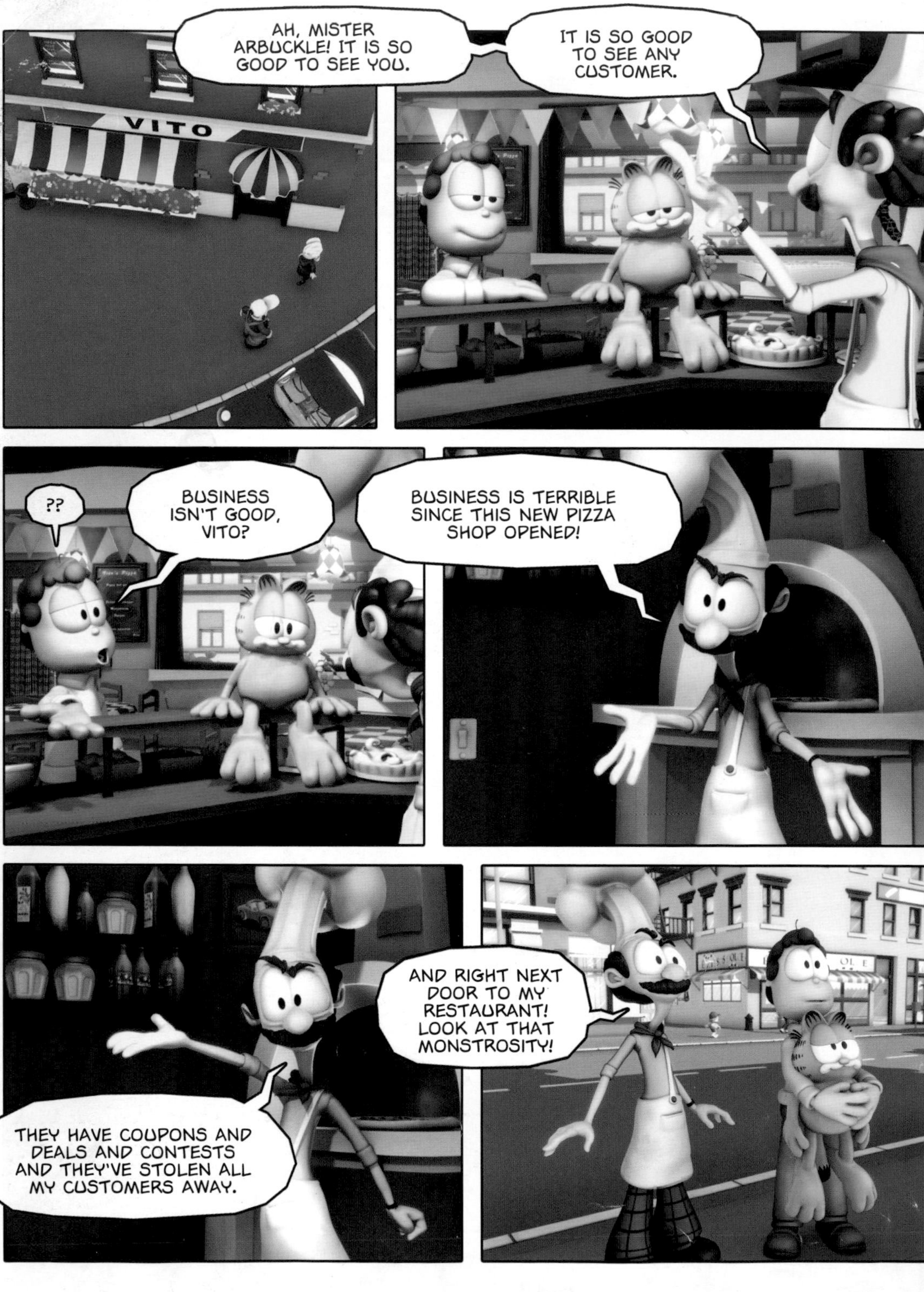
VITO
AH, MISTER ARBUCKLE! IT IS SO GOOD TO SEE YOU.
IT IS SO GOOD TO SEE ANY CUSTOMER.
??
BUSINESS ISN'T GOOD, VITO?
BUSINESS IS TERRIBLE SINCE THIS NEW PIZZA SHOP OPENED!
THEY HAVE COUPONS AND DEALS AND CONTESTS AND THEY'VE STOLEN ALL MY CUSTOMERS AWAY.
AND RIGHT NEXT DOOR TO MY RESTAURANT! LOOK AT THAT MONSTROSITY!

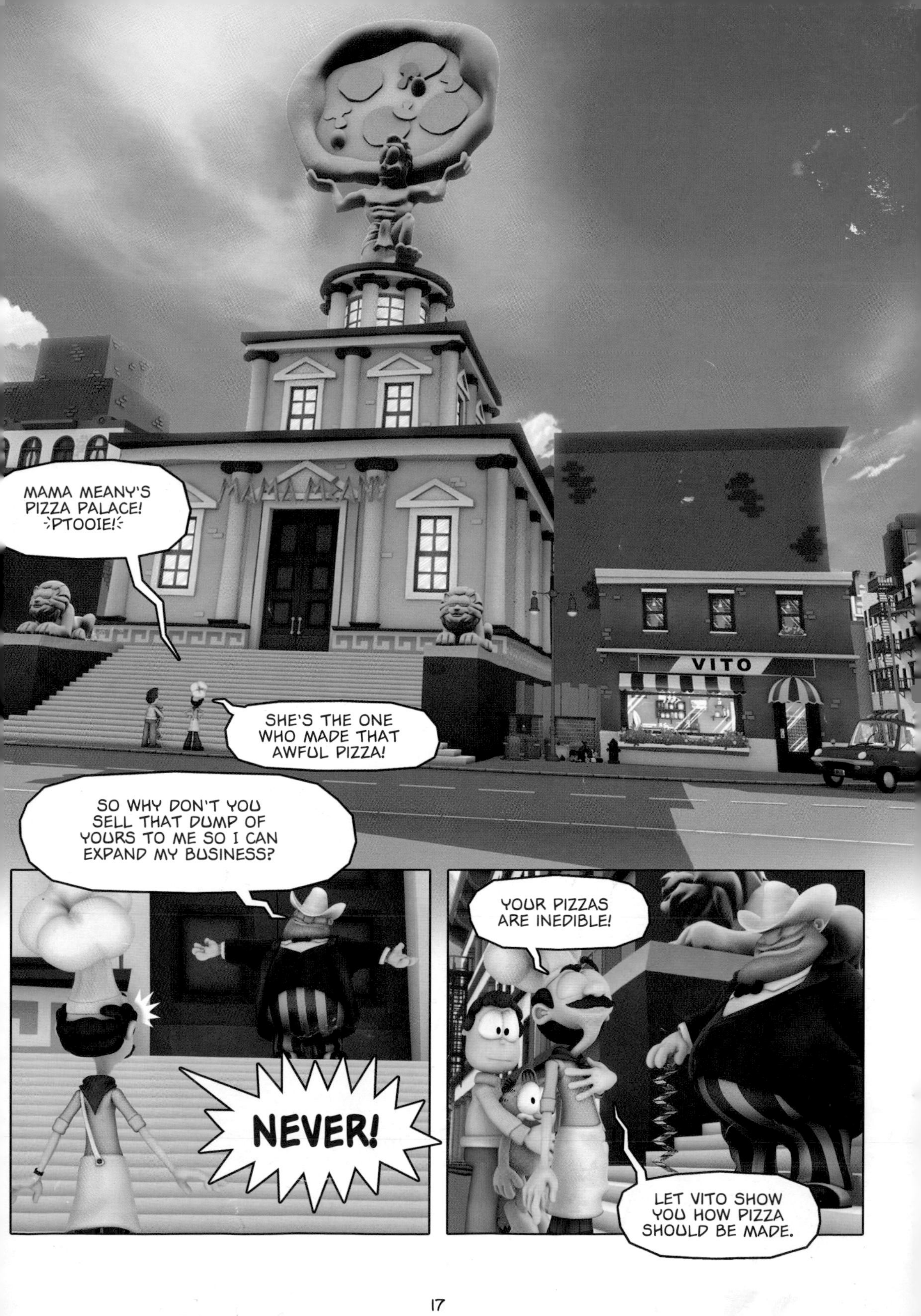

MAMA MEANY
VITO
MAMA MEANY'S PIZZA PALACE! PTOOIE!
SHE'S THE ONE WHO MADE THAT AWFUL PIZZA!
SO WHY DON'T YOU SELL THAT DUMP OF YOURS TO ME SO I CAN EXPAND MY BUSINESS?
NEVER!
YOUR PIZZAS ARE INEDIBLE!
LET VITO SHOW YOU HOW PIZZA SHOULD BE MADE.

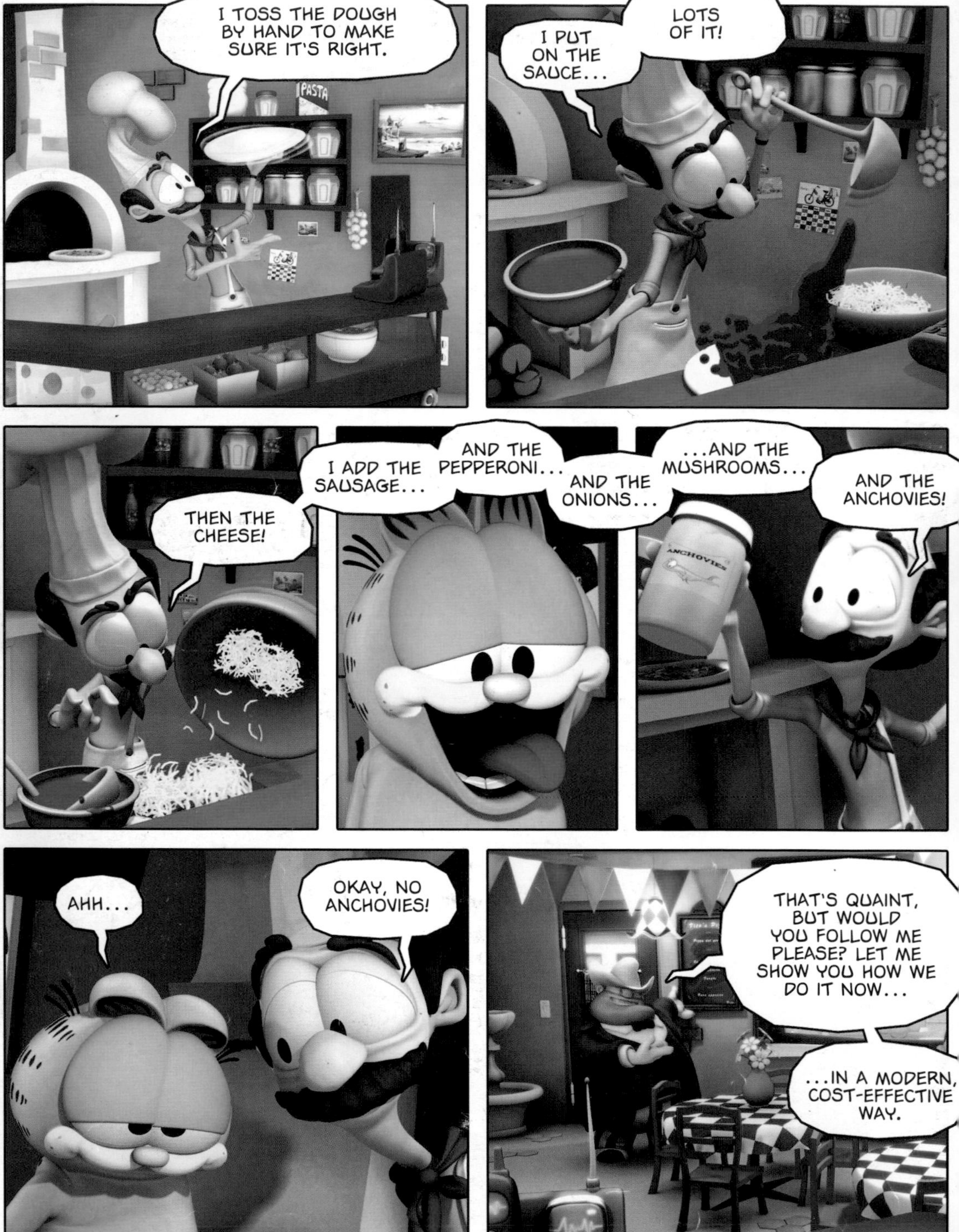
I TOSS THE DOUGH BY HAND TO MAKE SURE IT'S RIGHT.
PASTA
I PUT ON THE SAUCE...
LOTS OF IT!
THEN THE CHEESE!
I ADD THE SAUSAGE...
AND THE PEPPERONI...
AND THE ONIONS...
...AND THE MUSHROOMS...
AND THE ANCHOVIES!
ANCHOVIES
AHH...
OKAY, NO ANCHOVIES!
THAT'S QUAINT, BUT WOULD YOU FOLLOW ME PLEASE? LET ME SHOW YOU HOW WE DO IT NOW...
...IN A MODERN, COST-EFFECTIVE WAY.

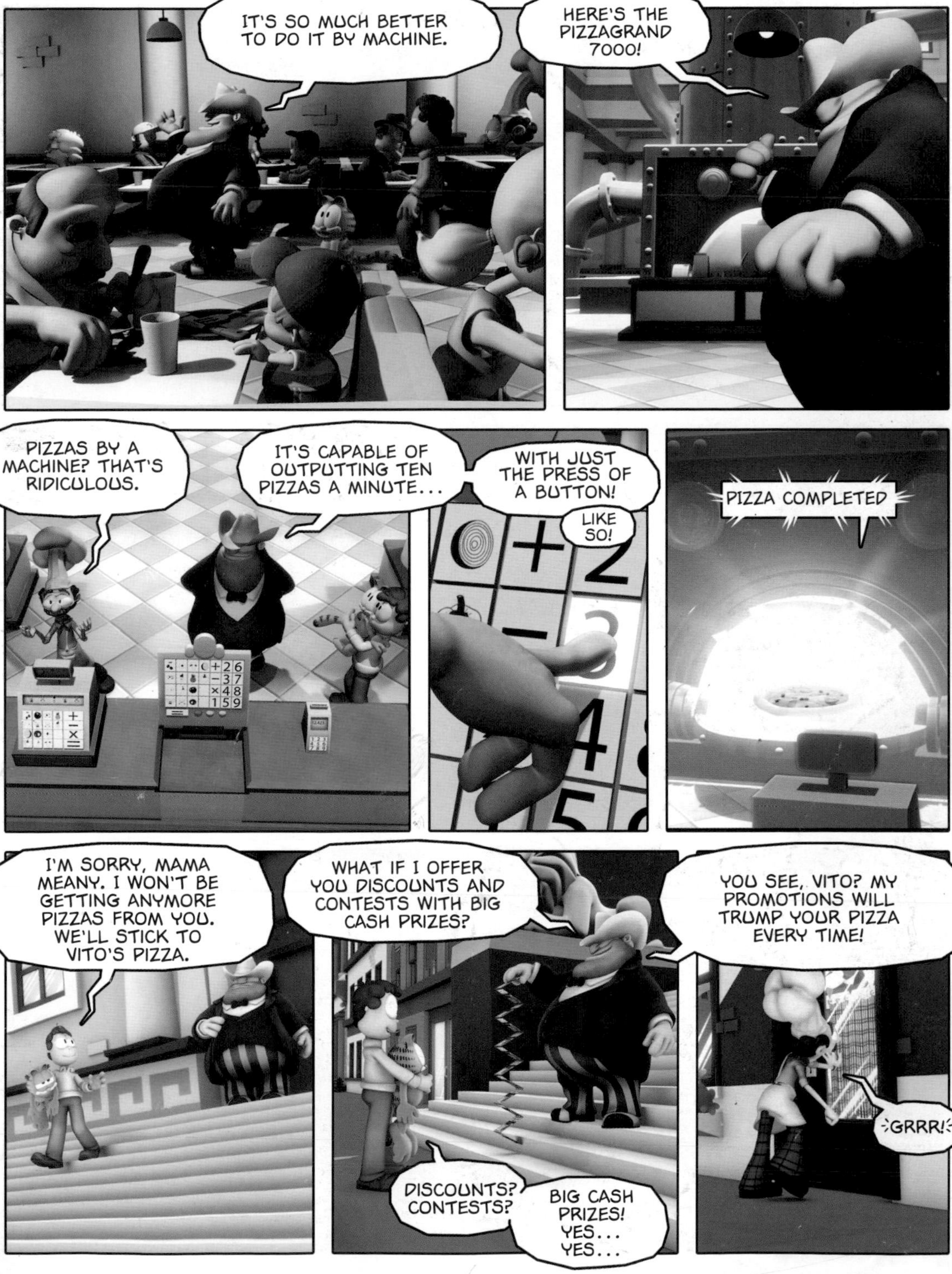
IT'S SO MUCH BETTER TO DO IT BY MACHINE.
HERE'S THE PIZZAGRAND 7000!
PIZZAS BY A MACHINE? THAT'S RIDICULOUS.
IT'S CAPABLE OF OUTPUTTING TEN PIZZAS A MINUTE...
WITH JUST THE PRESS OF A BUTTON!
LIKE SO!
PIZZA COMPLETED
I'M SORRY, MAMA MEANY. I WON'T BE GETTING ANYMORE PIZZAS FROM YOU. WE'LL STICK TO VITO'S PIZZA.
WHAT IF I OFFER YOU DISCOUNTS AND CONTESTS WITH BIG CASH PRIZES?
DISCOUNTS? CONTESTS?
BIG CASH PRIZES! YES... YES...
YOU SEE, VITO? MY PROMOTIONS WILL TRUMP YOUR PIZZA EVERY TIME!
GRRR!

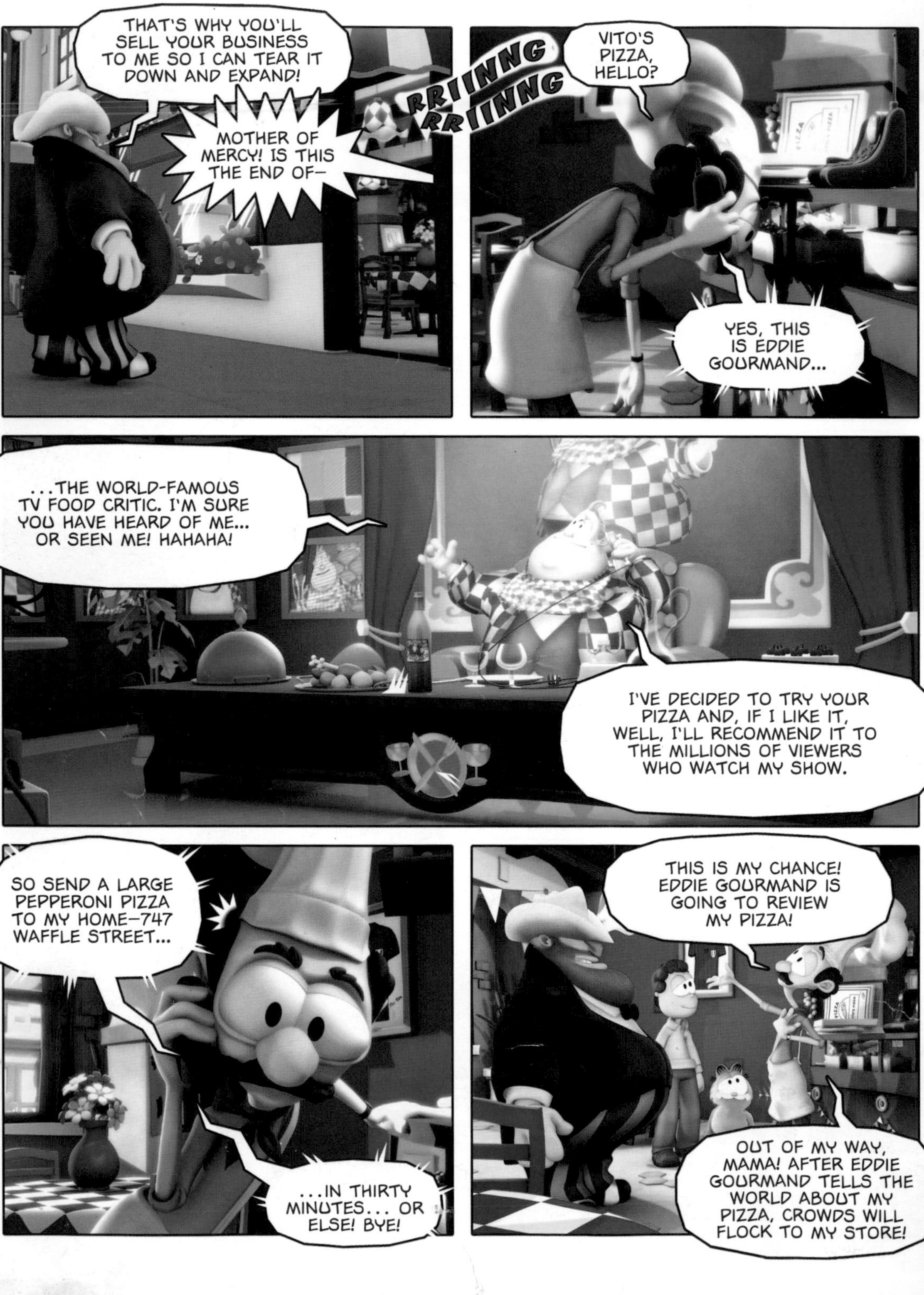
THAT'S WHY YOU'LL SELL YOUR BUSINESS TO ME SO I CAN TEAR IT DOWN AND EXPAND!
MOTHER OF MERCY! IS THIS THE END OF—
RRIIINNG RRIIINNG
VITO'S PIZZA, HELLO?
YES, THIS IS EDDIE GOURMAND...
...THE WORLD-FAMOUS TV FOOD CRITIC. I'M SURE YOU HAVE HEARD OF ME... OR SEEN ME! HAHAHA!
I'VE DECIDED TO TRY YOUR PIZZA AND, IF I LIKE IT, WELL, I'LL RECOMMEND IT TO THE MILLIONS OF VIEWERS WHO WATCH MY SHOW.
SO SEND A LARGE PEPPERONI PIZZA TO MY HOME—747 WAFFLE STREET...
...IN THIRTY MINUTES... OR ELSE! BYE!
THIS IS MY CHANCE! EDDIE GOURMAND IS GOING TO REVIEW MY PIZZA!
OUT OF MY WAY, MAMA! AFTER EDDIE GOURMAND TELLS THE WORLD ABOUT MY PIZZA, CROWDS WILL FLOCK TO MY STORE!

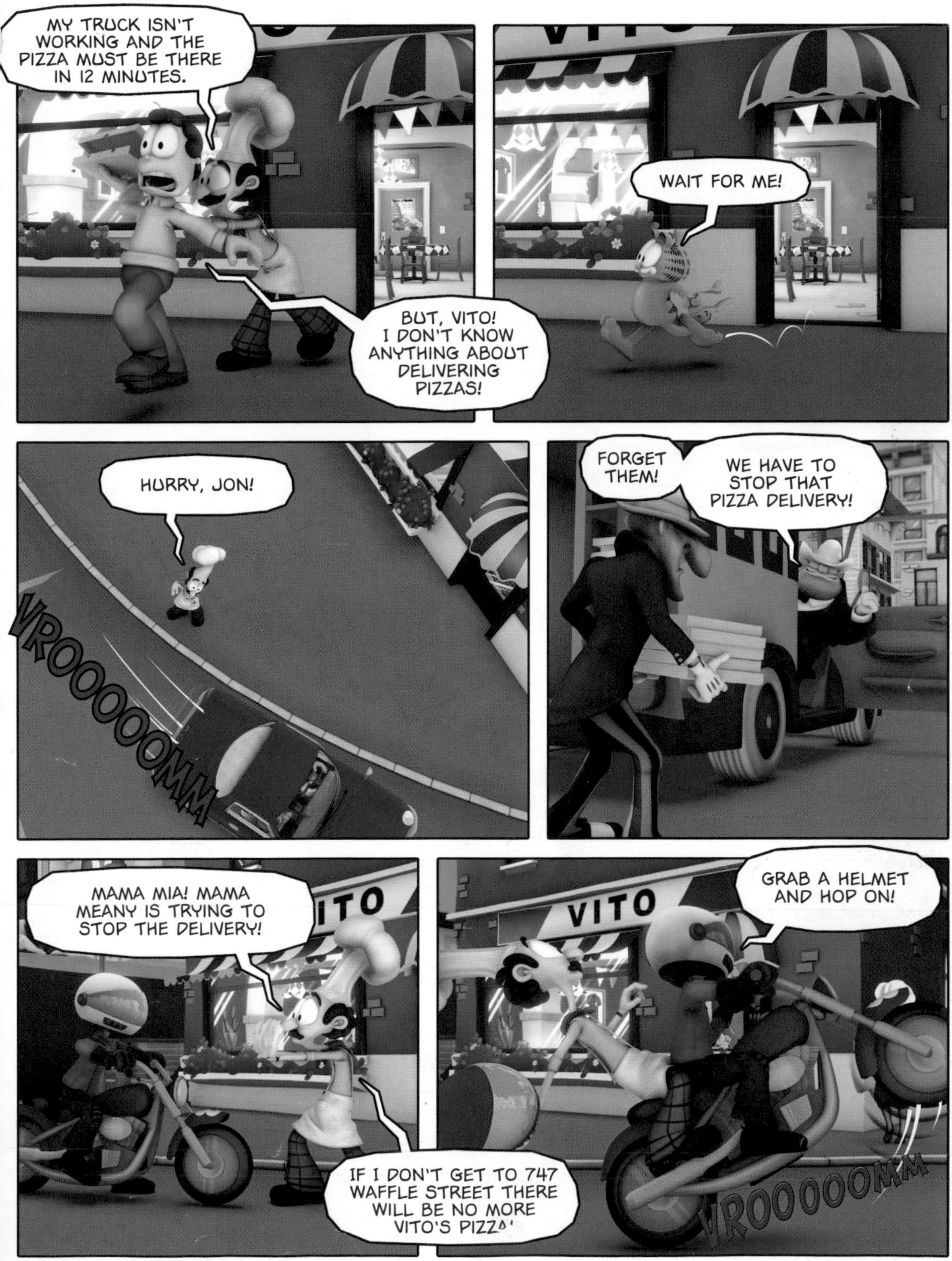
MY TRUCK ISN'T WORKING AND THE PIZZA MUST BE THERE IN 12 MINUTES.
BUT, VITO! I DON'T KNOW ANYTHING ABOUT DELIVERING PIZZAS!
WAIT FOR ME!
HURRY, JON!
VROOOOOOMM
FORGET THEM!
WE HAVE TO STOP THAT PIZZA DELIVERY!
VITO
MAMA MIA! MAMA MEANY IS TRYING TO STOP THE DELIVERY!
IF I DON'T GET TO 747 WAFFLE STREET THERE WILL BE NO MORE VITO'S PIZZA!
VITO
GRAB A HELMET AND HOP ON!
VROOOOOOMM

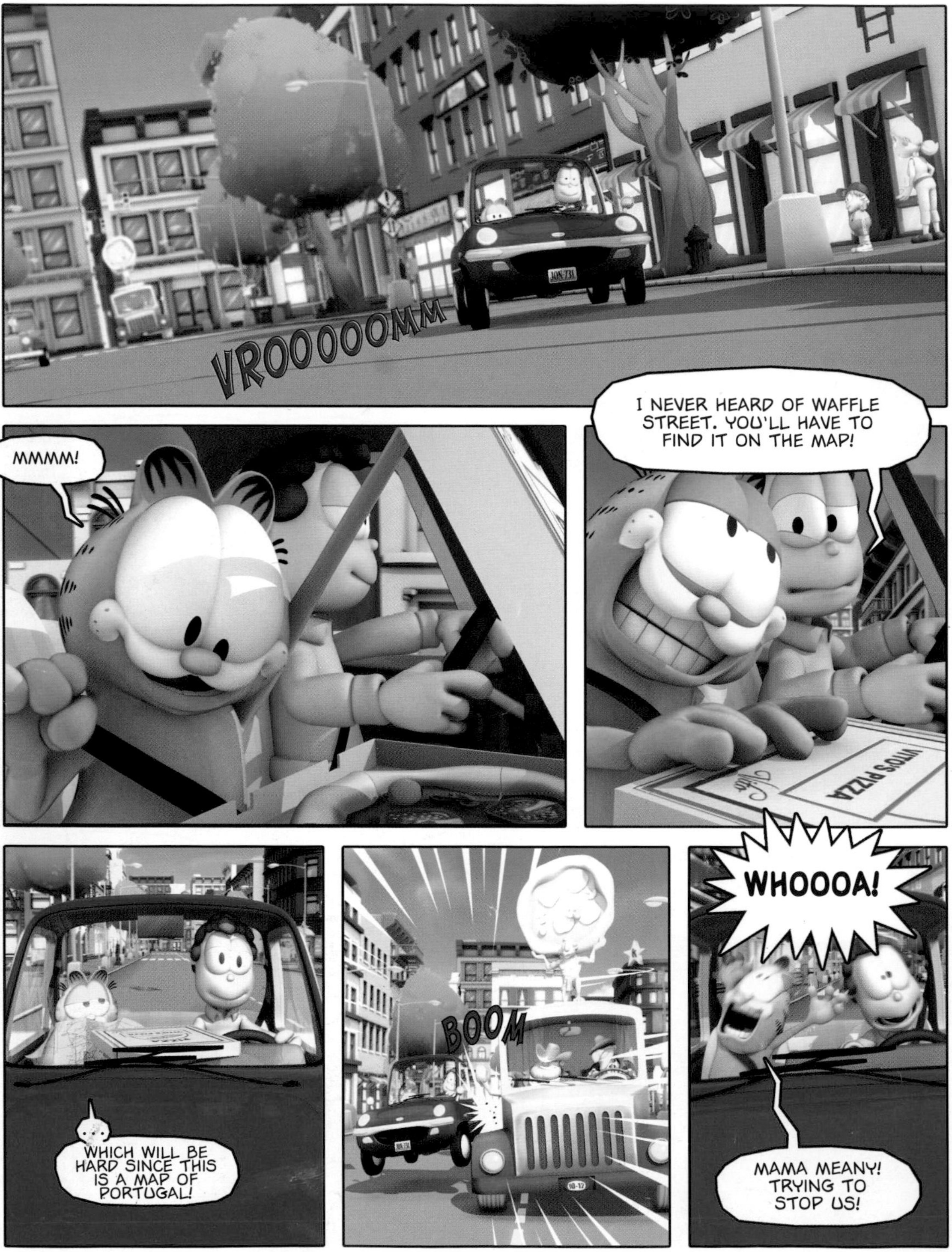
VROOOOOMM
MMMM!
I NEVER HEARD OF WAFFLE STREET. YOU'LL HAVE TO FIND IT ON THE MAP!
VITO'S PIZZA
WHICH WILL BE HARD SINCE THIS IS A MAP OF PORTUGAL!
BOOM
WHOOOA!
MAMA MEANY! TRYING TO STOP US!

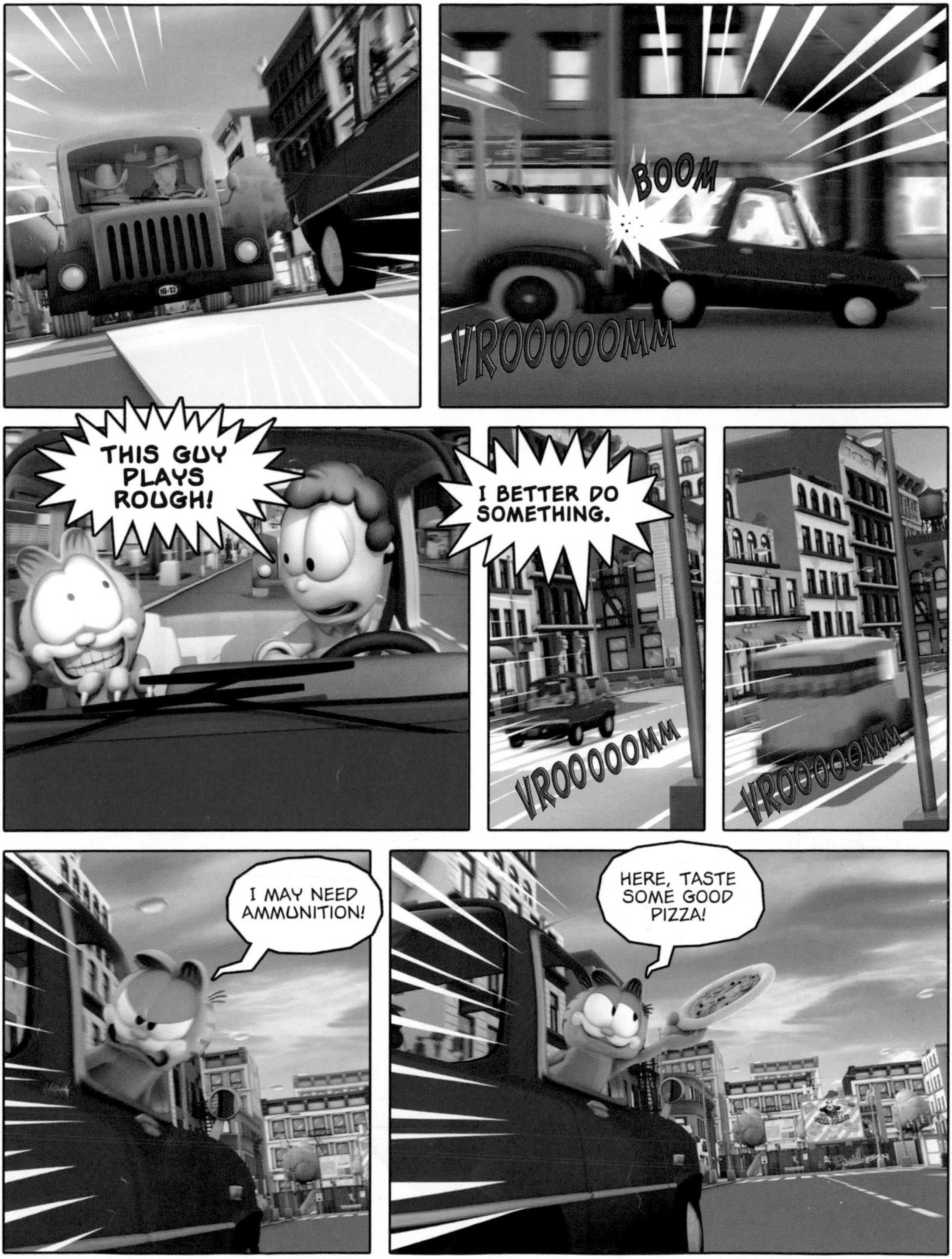
BOOM
VROOOOOMM
THIS GUY PLAYS ROUGH!
I BETTER DO SOMETHING.
VROOOOOMM
VROOOOOMM
I MAY NEED AMMUNITION!
HERE, TASTE SOME GOOD PIZZA!

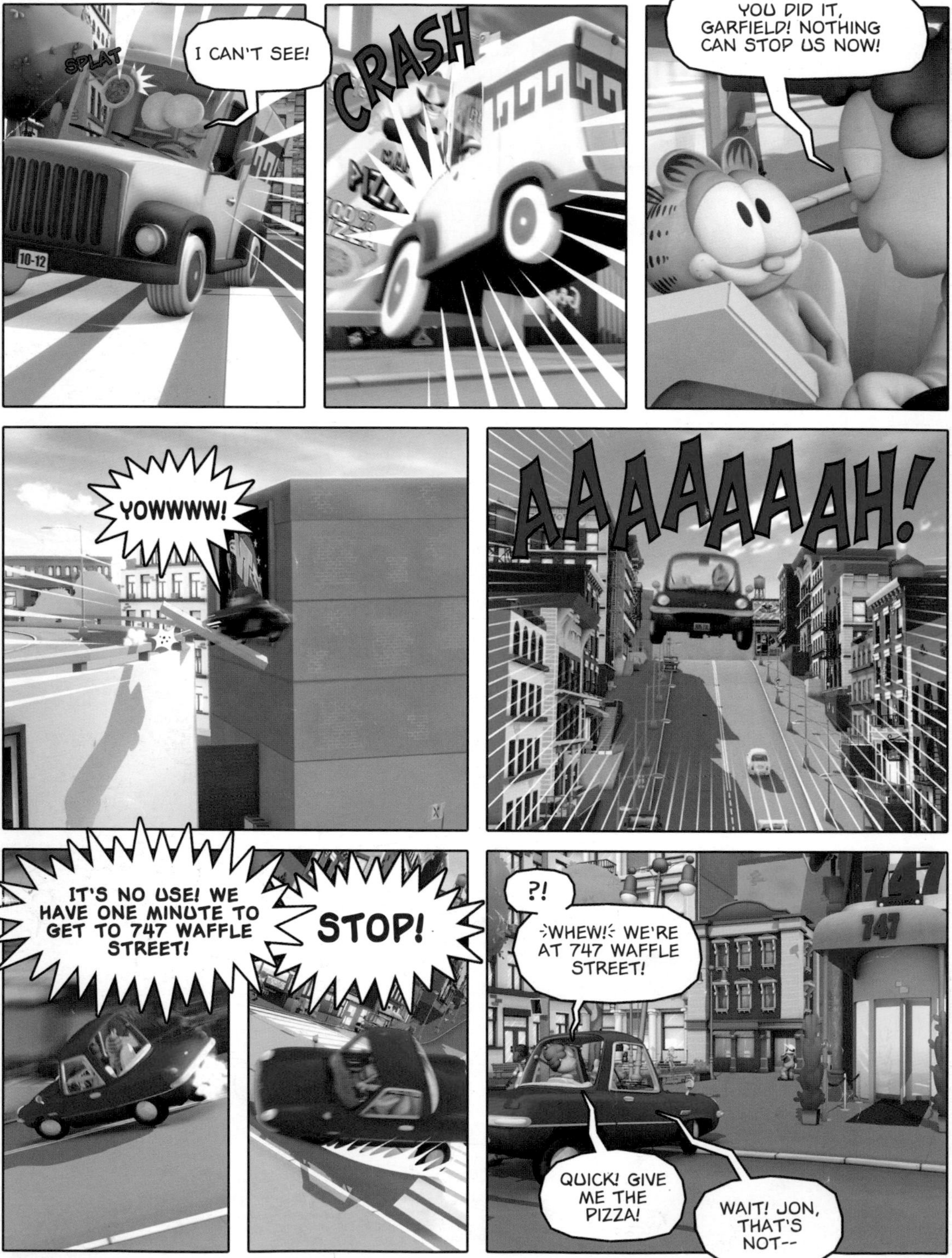
SPLAT
I CAN'T SEE!
CRASH
YOU DID IT, GARFIELD! NOTHING CAN STOP US NOW!
YOWWWW!
AAAAAAAH!
IT'S NO USE! WE HAVE ONE MINUTE TO GET TO 747 WAFFLE STREET!
STOP!
?!
WHEW! WE'RE AT 747 WAFFLE STREET!
QUICK! GIVE ME THE PIZZA!
WAIT! JON, THAT'S NOT--

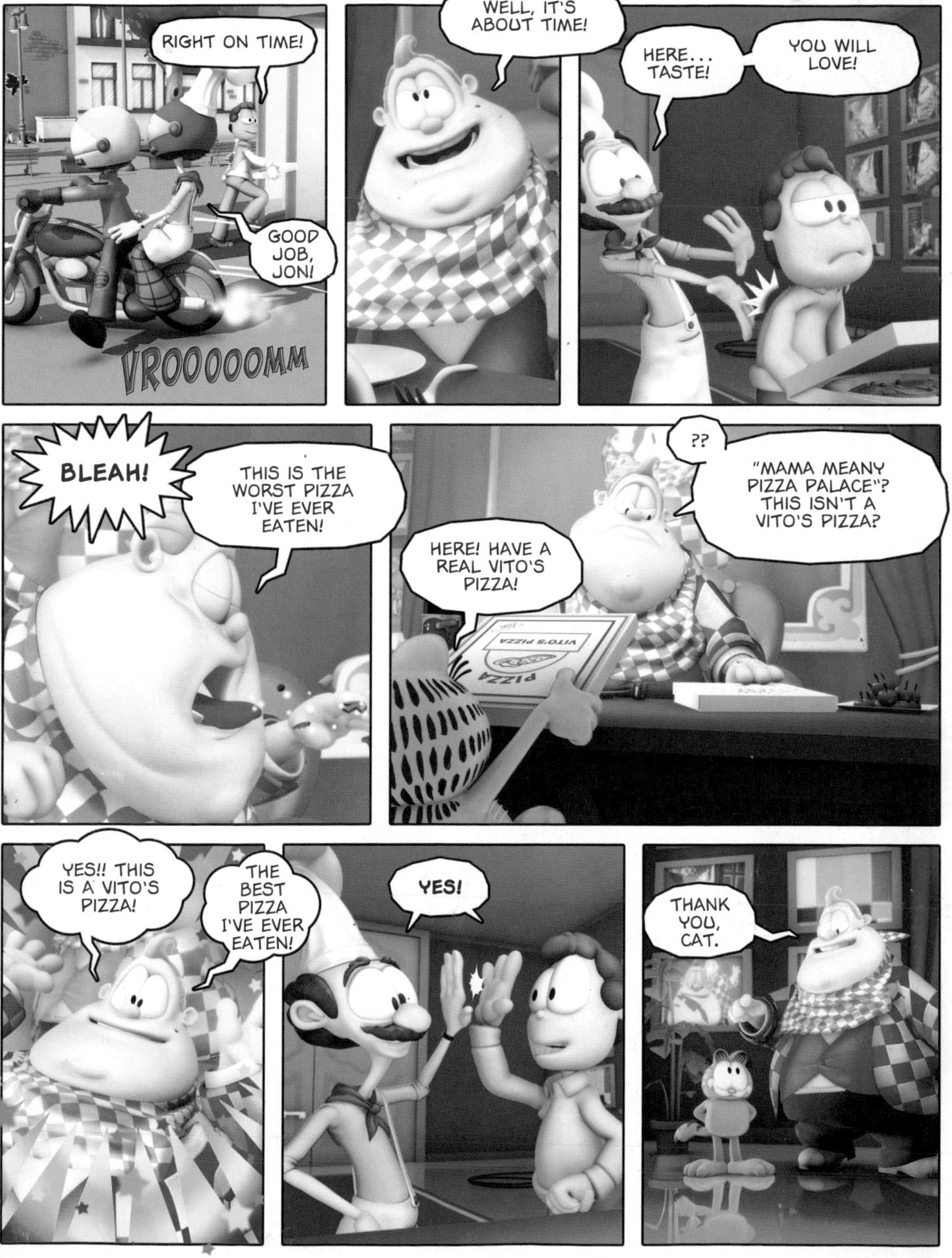
RIGHT ON TIME!
GOOD JOB, JON!
VROOOOOMM
WELL, IT'S ABOUT TIME!
HERE... TASTE!
YOU WILL LOVE!
BLEAH!
THIS IS THE WORST PIZZA I'VE EVER EATEN!
??
"MAMA MEANY PIZZA PALACE"? THIS ISN'T A VITO'S PIZZA?
HERE! HAVE A REAL VITO'S PIZZA!
VITO'S PIZZA
PIZZA
YES!! THIS IS A VITO'S PIZZA!
THE BEST PIZZA I'VE EVER EATEN!
YES!
THANK YOU, CAT.

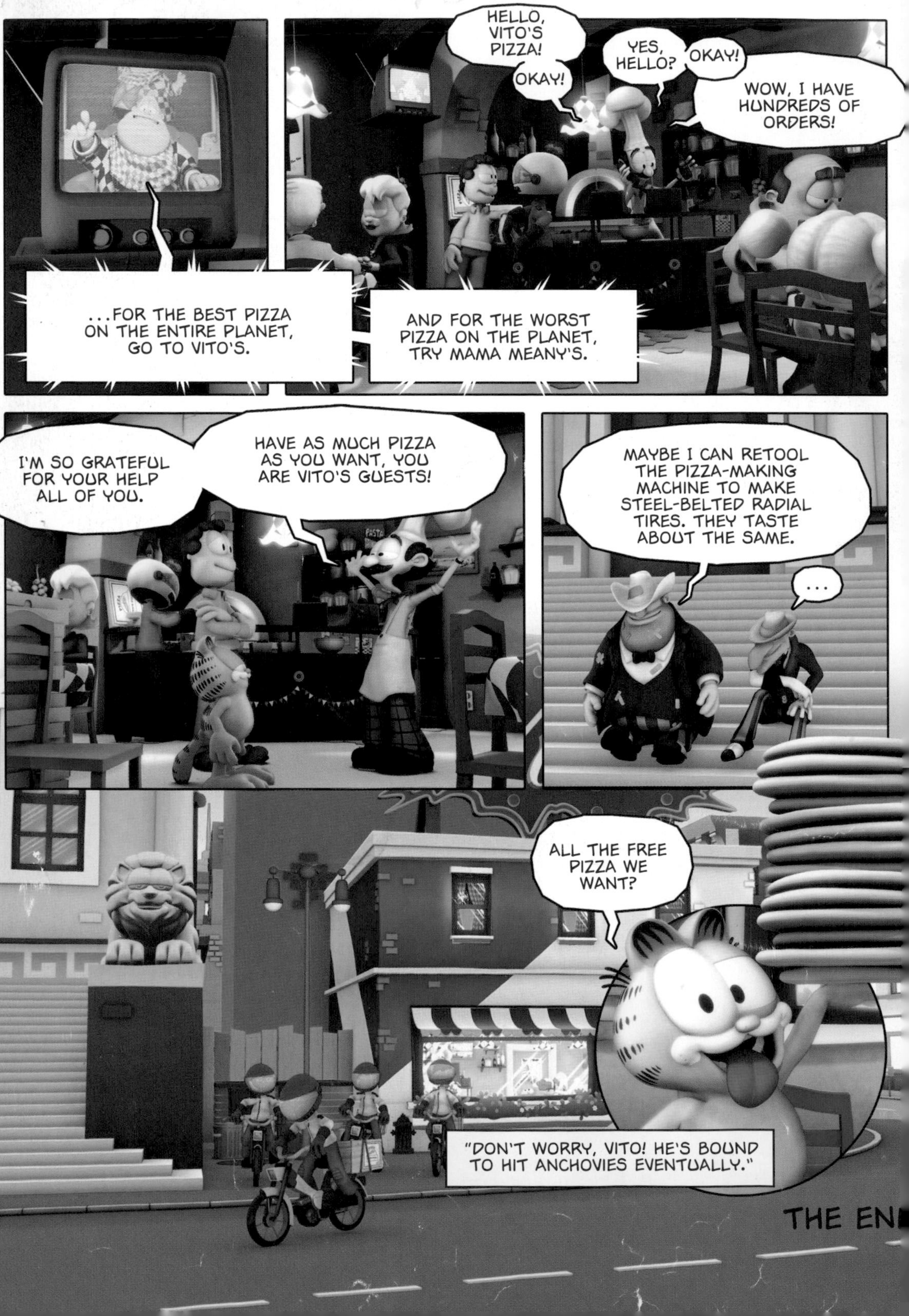
...FOR THE BEST PIZZA ON THE ENTIRE PLANET, GO TO VITO'S.
AND FOR THE WORST PIZZA ON THE PLANET, TRY MAMA MEANY'S.
HELLO, VITO'S PIZZA!
OKAY!
YES, HELLO?
OKAY!
WOW, I HAVE HUNDREDS OF ORDERS!
I'M SO GRATEFUL FOR YOUR HELP ALL OF YOU.
HAVE AS MUCH PIZZA AS YOU WANT, YOU ARE VITO'S GUESTS!
MAYBE I CAN RETOOL THE PIZZA-MAKING MACHINE TO MAKE STEEL-BELTED RADIAL TIRES. THEY TASTE ABOUT THE SAME.
...
ALL THE FREE PIZZA WE WANT?
"DON'T WORRY, VITO! HE'S BOUND TO HIT ANCHOVIES EVENTUALLY."
THE EN

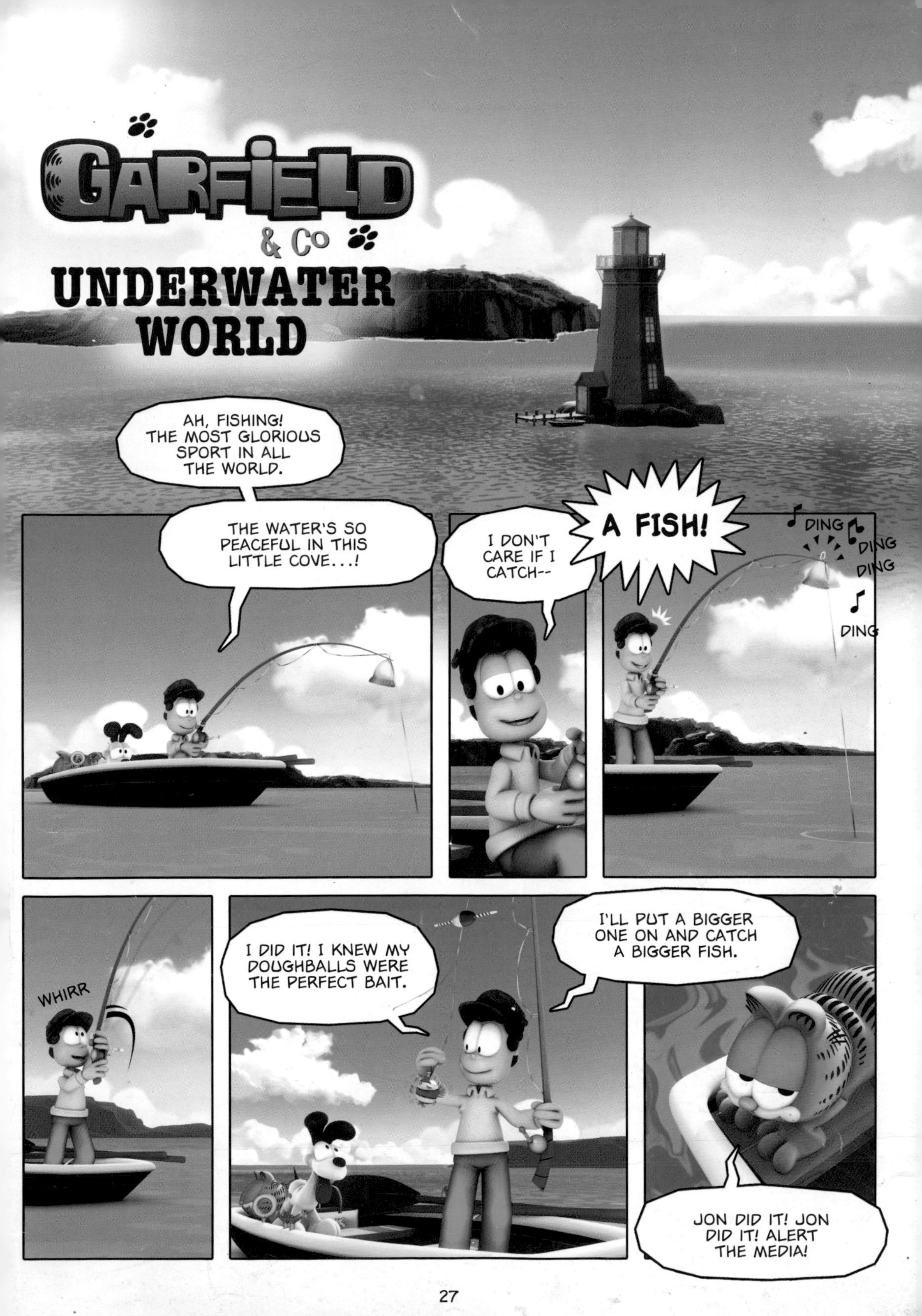
GARFIELD
& Co
UNDERWATER WORLD
AH, FISHING! THE MOST GLORIOUS SPORT IN ALL THE WORLD.
THE WATER'S SO PEACEFUL IN THIS LITTLE COVE...!
I DON'T CARE IF I CATCH--
A FISH!
DING DING DING DING
WHIRR
I DID IT! I KNEW MY DOUGHBALLS WERE THE PERFECT BAIT.
I'LL PUT A BIGGER ONE ON AND CATCH A BIGGER FISH.
JON DID IT! JON DID IT! ALERT THE MEDIA!

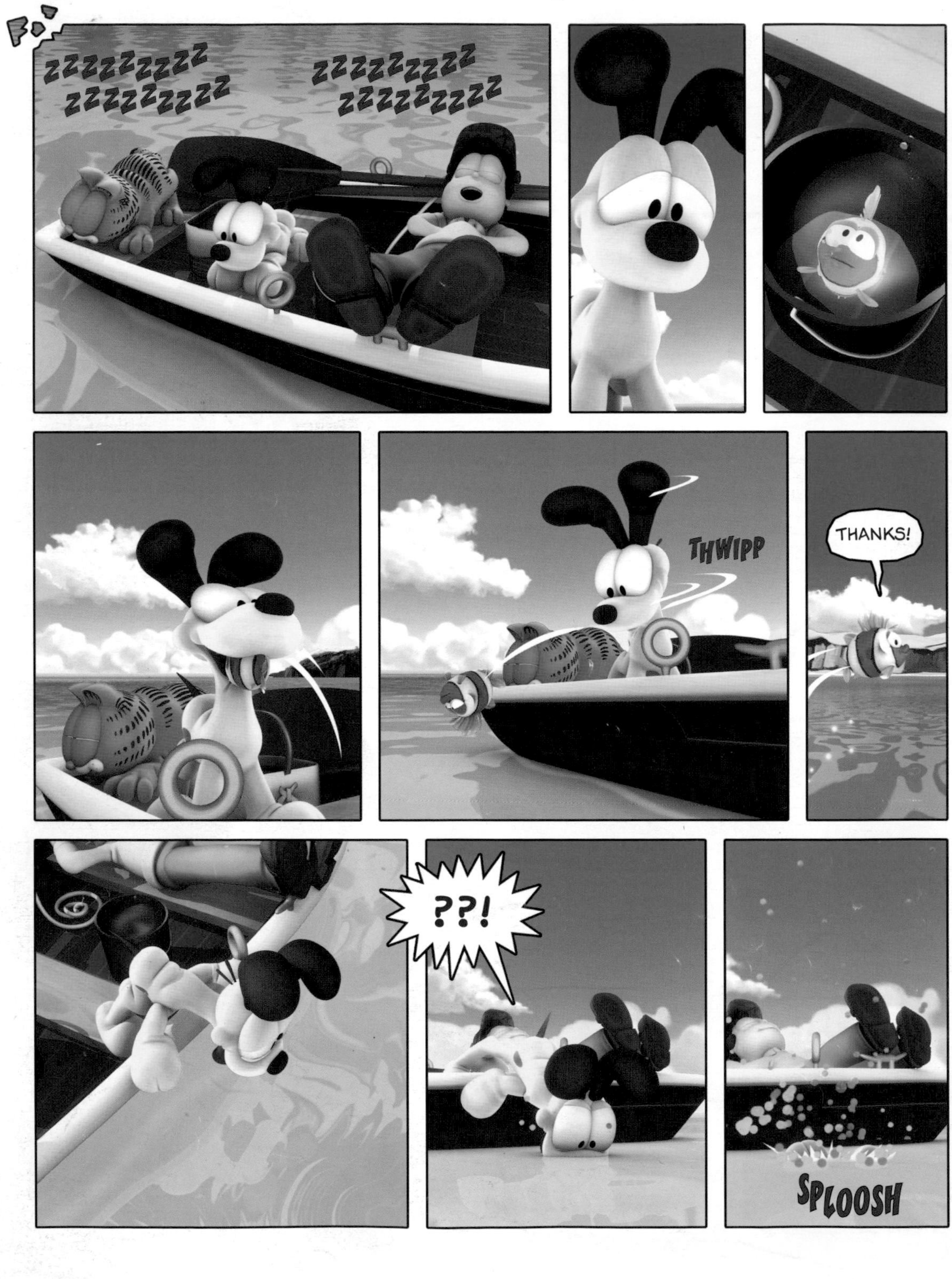
ZZZZZZZZZZ
ZZZZZZZZZZ
ZZZZZZZZZZ
ZZZZZZZZZZ
THWIPP
THANKS!
??!
SPLOOSH

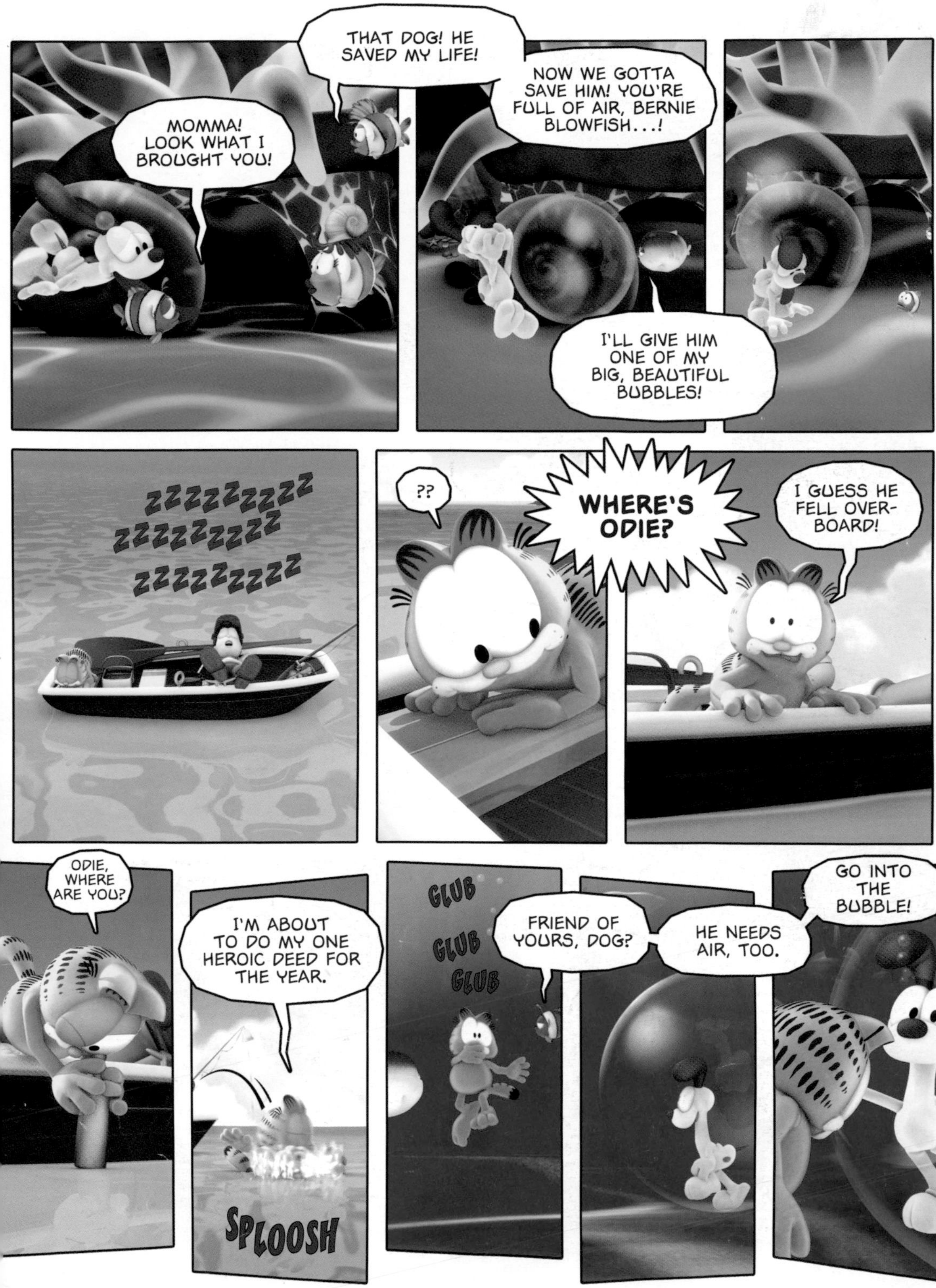
MOMMA! LOOK WHAT I BROUGHT YOU!
THAT DOG! HE SAVED MY LIFE!
NOW WE GOTTA SAVE HIM! YOU'RE FULL OF AIR, BERNIE BLOWFISH...!
I'LL GIVE HIM ONE OF MY BIG, BEAUTIFUL BUBBLES!
ZZZZZZZZZZ
ZZZZZZZZZZ
ZZZZZZZZZ
??
WHERE'S ODIE?
I GUESS HE FELL OVER-BOARD!
ODIE, WHERE ARE YOU?
I'M ABOUT TO DO MY ONE HEROIC DEED FOR THE YEAR.
SPLOOSH
GLUB
GLUB
GLUB
FRIEND OF YOURS, DOG?
HE NEEDS AIR, TOO.
GO INTO THE BUBBLE!

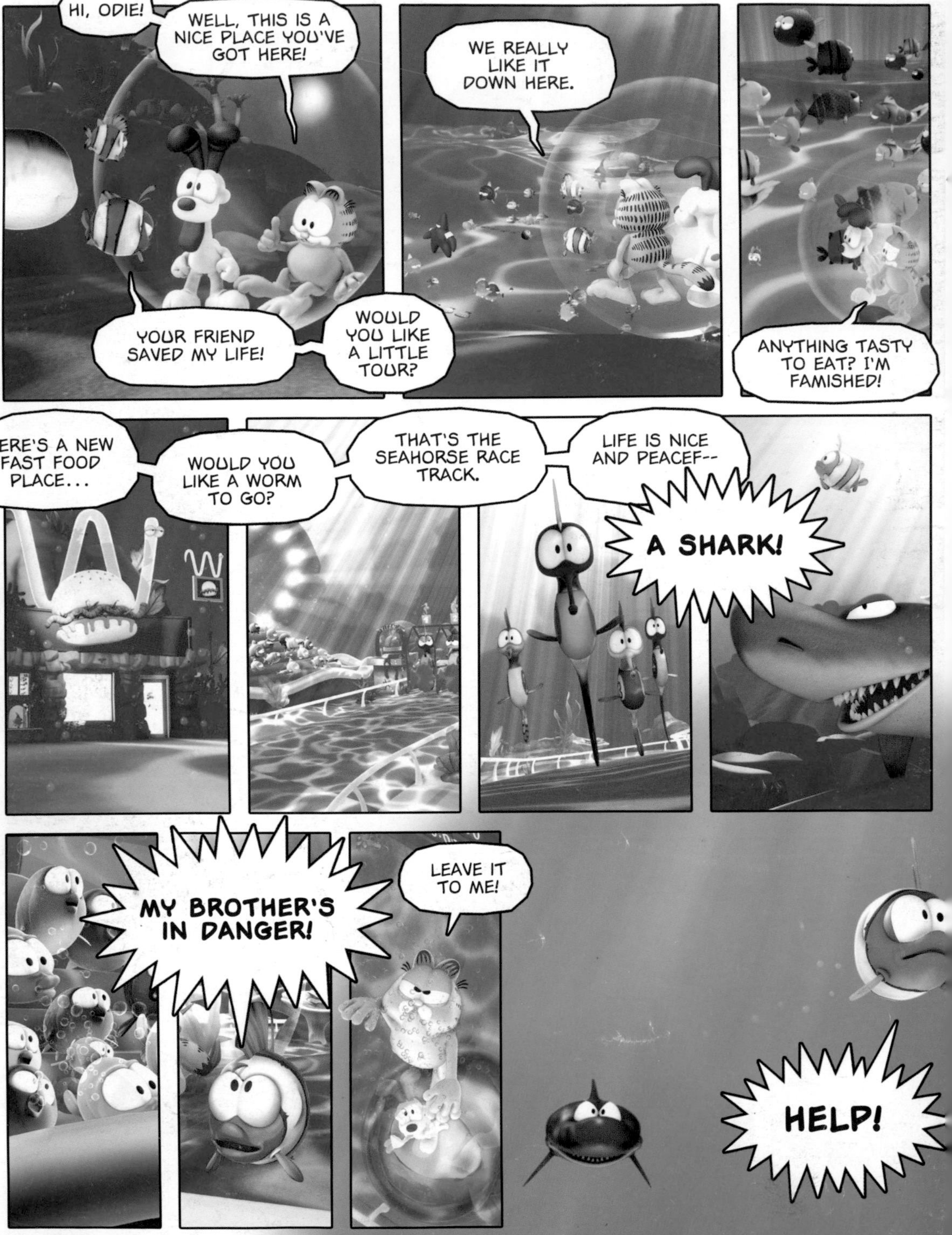

HI, ODIE!
WELL, THIS IS A NICE PLACE YOU'VE GOT HERE!
YOUR FRIEND SAVED MY LIFE!
WOULD YOU LIKE A LITTLE TOUR?
WE REALLY LIKE IT DOWN HERE.
ANYTHING TASTY TO EAT? I'M FAMISHED!
HERE'S A NEW FAST FOOD PLACE...
WOULD YOU LIKE A WORM TO GO?
THAT'S THE SEAHORSE RACE TRACK.
LIFE IS NICE AND PEACEF--
A SHARK!
MY BROTHER'S IN DANGER!
LEAVE IT TO ME!
HELP!

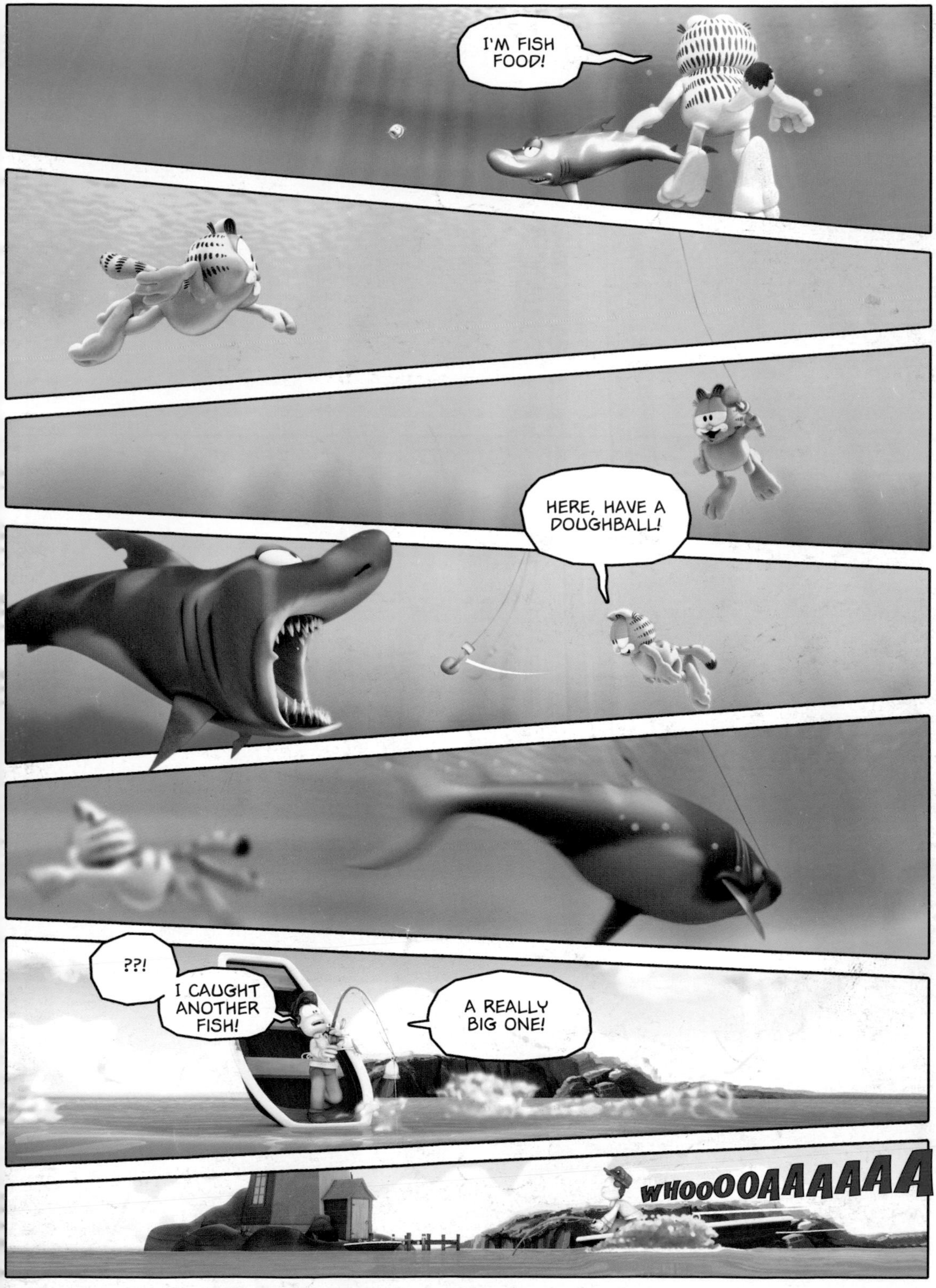

I'M FISH FOOD!
HERE, HAVE A DOUGHBALL!
??!
I CAUGHT ANOTHER FISH!
A REALLY BIG ONE!
WHOOOOOAAAAAA

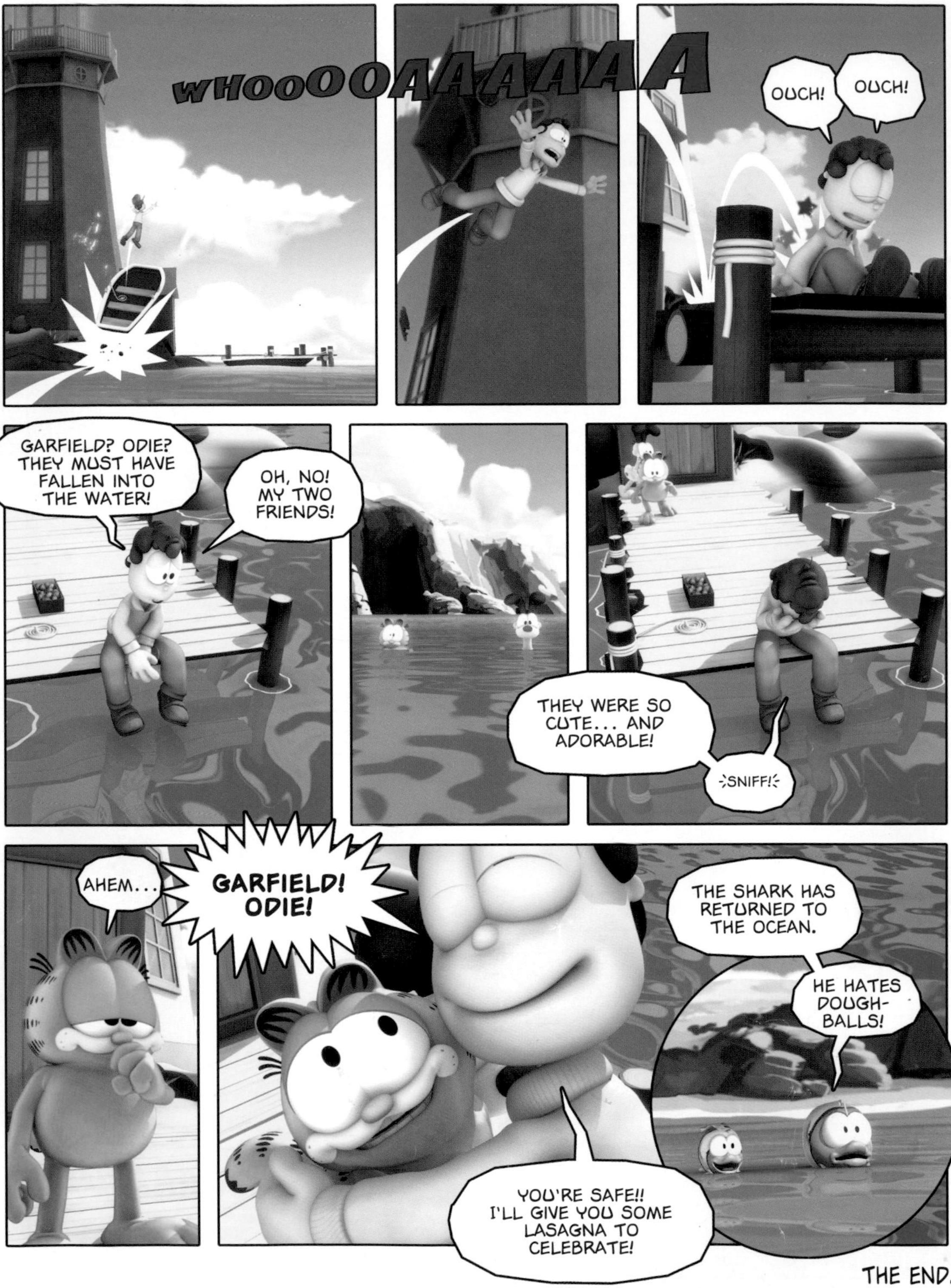
WHOOOOOAAAAAAA
OUCH!
OUCH!
GARFIELD? ODIE? THEY MUST HAVE FALLEN INTO THE WATER!
OH, NO! MY TWO FRIENDS!
THEY WERE SO CUTE... AND ADORABLE!
SNIFF!
AHEM...
GARFIELD! ODIE!
THE SHARK HAS RETURNED TO THE OCEAN.
HE HATES DOUGH-BALLS!
YOU'RE SAFE!! I'LL GIVE YOU SOME LASAGNA TO CELEBRATE!

THE END.